*Totally Bound Publishing books by Helena Maeve:*

A Touch of Spice
Courting Treason
Collision Course
Misfit Hearts
Eden's Embers
Flight Made Easy
In the Presence of Mine Enemy
Fault Lines
Feint and Misdirection
Glass Houses

**Surface Tension**
Twice Upon a Blue Moon

**Anthologies**
Wild Angels: Grounds for Divorce

Surface Tension

# TWICE UPON A BLUE MOON

HELENA MAEVE

Twice Upon a Blue Moon
ISBN # 978-1-78430-523-9
©Copyright Helena Maeve 2015
Cover Art by Posh Gosh ©Copyright March 2015
Interior text design by Claire Siemaszkiewicz
Totally Bound Publishing

# TWICE UPON A BLUE MOON

# Chapter One

The dashboard clock read one fifty-two. Sadie's hour had elapsed by two minutes. There was no sign of her when Hazel glanced in the side mirror. She craned her neck over the seat, ignoring the frayed upholstery as she often did, just in case the angle of the mirror was playing tricks. No such luck. The rain-spattered sidewalk was bare of pedestrians.

Across the street, four-seven-one Aulden Way loomed like the homeless — half menacingly lost in shadow, half dolefully run-down.

Hazel drew her lower lip between her teeth. It was just two minutes. Sadie probably got distracted, or maybe adventure time with Mr. Tall, Dark and Handsome ran over schedule.

Or, failing that, she was already dead and the longer Hazel dawdled, the more time Tall, Dark and Handsome had to dispose of the body. Her insides roiled at the thought. *Too much* CSI. Sadie's track record with men slanted more toward the chronically unable to commit than the Norman Bates types.

*Sadie's probably fine,* Hazel told herself. The upholstery screeched as she twisted away.

She made a valiant attempt to turn back to her book, defying the kernel of panic blooming in her gut. Her eyes had just begun to glaze over the spidery print when a door clanged open somewhere behind the car.

Hazel twisted in her seat, paperback flying from her hands to nestle somewhere on the floor of the Volvo. A huddled pair stood outside number four-seven-one, zipping up their jackets as they conversed in low voices. Hazel took in their beanies and distressed, low-slung jeans and glanced away again. *Too short, too frumpy. No ankle-breaking stilettos.*

Hazel settled back in the seat, heart in her throat and hand on the pepper spray can dangling from the car key. The pair neared at a sluggish pace until eventually they passed the Volvo. They were holding hands.

Hazel watched them until they disappeared from view. Then she tore the keys out of the ignition and shoved open the car door. Instantly, the night chill rushed in to meet her. She stomped her way to the brownstone with a shiver as the icy wind seeped under her clothes. The denim jacket was poor cover from the cold front that had rolled in over the city.

*At least it's stopped raining.* She tested the front door. *Small mercies.* The door swung open with the barest nudge.

Two, three years ago, easy entry into an apartment building on this street would've been unthinkable. *Long live the yuppies and their cash.* Security cameras glared down at her from the ceiling. The hallway lamps all worked, too, progressively casting their warm glow over bare brick walls as Hazel started up the stairs. She couldn't see more than the next story up, but the motion sensors faithfully tracked her steps until she hit the third floor.

Sadie had mentioned that Tall, Dark and Handsome lived in three-B. Judging by the lettering on the doorbell, he also went by 'Best'. Hazel folded her fingers around the pepper spray can as she raised her other fist to the metal door.

Two loud raps tolled like claps of thunder. She winced with each one.

Seconds passed before the door clanged and unlatched. A dark-haired man stood in the gap wearing dark slacks and a white shirt—a Hugo Boss magazine spread made flesh. He cocked his head, gaze gliding down her body. "Can I…help you?"

He didn't seem to know what to do with Hazel's jean and jean outfit. Good. She was the Hardy to Sadie's Laurel, except blonde and pear-shaped. Where Sadie was slim and angular, Hazel strongly identified with the titular character in *Kung-Fu Panda*.

She could and would gladly sit on Mr. Best if he tried to stand in her way.

"Hazel!" Sadie's voice rang out from somewhere inside the loft. She came into view a moment later, hopping on one foot as she struggled to slot her red pump onto the other. "Hey. What're you doin' here?" Whenever she let her guard down, Sadie's accent came through loud and clear. Hazel could practically smell the hay bales.

Hazel tried not to squirm under their combined scrutiny. "It's been an hour." *You were taking too long.*

Best backed out of the doorway with a flourish. "Would you like to come in?" He flicked a hand in invitation, a soft smile playing across his bowed lips. "I make excellent margaritas."

"No, thanks. I'm only here to pick her up."

"Ah."

Sadie finally got her shoes on. "Sorry, we kinda lost track of time." She pulled down the hem of her leather skirt. She didn't seem to be sporting any bruises. "Didn't we, darlin'?" Her dimpled smiles were known for melting hearts. It was a shame Sadie had a habit of squandering them on useless tools who never seemed to treat her right.

"It was an absolute pleasure," Best replied. The kiss he planted on Sadie's temple was tender enough to make Hazel want to look away. She didn't.

Sadie giggled girlishly and slithered out of his arms. "Maybe I'll see you around?"

"You have my number." Best trained a pair of chocolate brown eyes on Hazel. "Maybe next time you'll come in for a drink... I didn't catch your name."

"I didn't give it."

Hazel started for the stairs, content to disregard Sadie's scandalized expression. She heard her apologize as she pushed past the door of the brownstone.

Sadie caught up to her on the sidewalk. "What the hell was that?"

"What did you want me to say? Sure, we'll have that threesome you're fantasizing about?"

"Oh my God," Sadie groaned. "When did he say that?"

"Did you miss the part where he was flirting with me while you were standing right fucking there?"

"He was just being nice," Sadie scoffed, flinging her hands up to the heavens.

Hazel did her best to ignore Sadie as she slid behind the wheel. It was too cold and too late to shout at each other in the street. Sadie slammed the passenger side door shut as she climbed in.

"Why do you have to be such a weirdo about this stuff?"

"Really?" Hazel deadpanned. "You're really going to ask me that?"

Battle-frenzy fled Sadie's eyes. She tugged a hand through her curly blonde hair. "You know I didn't mean it like that. I just... I had fun, okay? He's a nice guy."

"Does that mean you'll call him?"

On this point, their opinions diverged dramatically. Sadie was a subscriber to the 'sorry, I forgot' school of public relations. She had a habit of stringing men along, even when they were nice and fun – and cool to be with.

True to form, she shrugged. "Maybe. Unless he actually *was* angling for a threesome."

Hazel keyed the engine. "You really had a good time?"

"I can give you details –"

"God, no. I'd have to bleach my ears," Hazel retorted, wrinkling her nose.

Sadie propped her knees against the dash. "Oh, come on. You have to admit you found him at least a little bit cute."

Despite herself, Hazel thought back to the dress shirt and iron-creased pants, the short, slicked-back black hair. "If you're into the *Wolf of Wall Street* look, I guess."

"You should see his playroom..." Sadie let out a wistful breath. "I could sleep for days after that."

"Good luck getting Marco to agree."

Sadie let her head fall back against the seat. "Marco loves me." She sounded a little out of it.

Hazel shot her a sidelong glance as they idled at a stoplight. Sadie's eyes were barely open, her features soft and relaxed, the way she normally got after smoking a bowl.

Something like jealousy curdled in Hazel's gut. Why couldn't she have that?

The answer rose up with the blinding memory of camera flashes and the dense perfume of spilled tequila.

"It's green," Sadie muttered.

"Right." Hazel put the Volvo into gear. They drove on.

* * * *

The Monday to Friday crowds had thinned significantly by Saturday morning, so Hazel put in a good word with Marco when she got in, then called Sadie to let her know she was taking her shift.

"You're the best," Sadie slurred into the phone.

"Drink lots of water," Hazel said and hung up.

"She sick?" Marco asked as he flipped pancakes in a battered skillet. "My sister's come down with something again. Says I can't bring Maria over or she'll catch the bug."

"Your sister has a very delicate constitution."

Hazel had met her once, after Marco's divorce had gone through and his whole family had temporarily relocated to the diner in the guise of emotional support. Free food was just a bonus. His sister was a head taller with fists the size of anvils. She did not strike Hazel as the kind of woman who suffered flu vectors easily.

Marco snickered. He had a very particular way of laughing, mostly through his nose and jerking his head back the way a bird might do before putting out an eye with its beak. "Seriously," Marco pressed. "Is she sick? I make a mean chicken soup…"

He was so painfully earnest that Hazel wanted to hug him.

As long as she'd been working at the diner, his steadfast affection for Sadie had remained constant. It was something of an open secret that he had only hired Hazel on her say-so. He had overlooked a lean résumé and offered her a helping hand when she was sinking.

Hazel was grateful to him, but not enough to keep from editing the truth.

"She's just hung over." *From getting her brains fucked out by Mr. Best.* "I'll go see if anyone needs a refill." She flitted out of the kitchen before Marco could press her for details.

Out front, the regular early birds were largely absent. Hazel recognized a couple of high school kids from the nearby development, earphones thrust in and fingers flying over the keyboards of their iPads. Their burgundy and gray uniforms gave them away. Hazel circled around their booth, working her way around the occupied tables. By the window, a taxi driver who stopped in after every graveyard shift looked up from his newspaper when Hazel topped off his coffee.

"What's new, Allan?" A nondescript name for a nondescript, blond face. Hazel wouldn't have known he used to be an Olympic gymnast if she hadn't heard it straight from the horse's mouth.

The cabbie rolled his shoulders, joints creaking like misaligned metal rods. "Got another ticket last night. Swear the cops have it in for me."

"It's Orange County," Hazel pointed out. "They have it in for everyone below the poverty line." She patted his shoulder with a companionable hand. "I'll go see about your pancakes."

"I didn't order any."

"Then who...?" Hazel tracked Allan's rheumy gaze to a stooped figure in the booth at the back. "Oh. Thanks."

"Wouldn't say no to pancakes on the house, though!" she heard Allan heckle.

Her attention was diverted by the crisp collar of the man poring over his cell phone at the rear of the diner. She didn't recognize him until he glanced up.

"I know what you're thinking," Best started with a beatific smile. "Of all the gin joints..."

"More like 'pretty sure this counts as stalking'."

Best's smile dimmed like a switch had been flipped. "Is Sadie around?"

"She's not working this morning."

"Is she all right?" Best leaned an arm against the back of the booth, his Rolex resting awkwardly on cerise vinyl. He dropped his voice an octave. "Is it because of...last night?"

Hazel white-knuckled the coffeepot handle. It was tempting to say *Yes, you screwed her up and now she's a weepy mess. Yes, you should've asked her to stay the night.* She recognized that thread of malice that wound around her thoughts. It was familiar cruelty.

"No."

Best heaved a breath, shoulders sagging a little. "Oh. Good." He sounded genuinely relieved.

"You want more coffee?" Hazel asked, swirling her pot.

"Yes, thank you..." Best maneuvered his mug to the edge of the table so she could fill it. His fingers were very pale around the ceramic—nails square and neatly trimmed, not a hangnail or callus in sight.

*No wonder.* He probably hadn't worked an honest day in his life.

"Look. You do what you want, but Sadie said she'll call you," Hazel recalled. "You don't need to show up here to pressure her."

"It's a free country."

Hazel shrugged, trying to play off the venom that rose to the tip of her tongue. "That's why I said do what you want." *You will, anyway.* Men like Best talked a good game about fairness when it suited them but at the end of the day, they only saw to their own bottom line. She knew the type. She'd spent three years kowtowing for scraps from a man none too different.

"Are you this friendly to all of Sadie's boyfriends?"

"Wasn't aware you were her boyfriend." *Were,* not *are.* Hazel couldn't snuff out a flicker of pride for chasing vernacular out of her repertoire when faced with the likes of Best.

Best sucked his cheeks in, as though to conceal a smile. "Touché. I suppose I'm not. But still. Can't help feel there's something about me you don't like."

"Oh, don't lose sleep over it. I bet I'm not the only one."

"I won't."

*Jerk.*

She felt Best's gaze on her back as she sauntered away to retrieve his pancakes. It stirred something akin to panic in her belly, but Hazel knew how to shove past bothersome discomfort.

The swinging kitchen doors made for a paltry shield.

"So tell me more about your sister," she entreated, before Marco could ask about Sadie.

By the time she returned to his table with the pancakes, Best was on the phone. He met her eyes for a moment, smiled apologetically, and returned to his hums and hmphs. Hazel made a point not to feel affronted. There were worse things on this job than being ignored.

Marco kept her from dwelling with tales about his sister's vacation in the Caribbean where purportedly she had fought off a real, live shark and lived to tell the tale.

"And that's how she got a bionic thumb—" Marco jerked his chin to the horseshoe of Formica tables fanned around the diner. "Did you get his check?"

Hazel turned just as the door of the diner clanged shut. Best's retreating back flashed into view for a breath then was gone, swallowed up by the swarm of pedestrians on their way to the department stores and food courts that served organic vegetables and lactose-free salad dressing. "Shit."

"It's coming out of your paycheck," Marco remarked in a singsong, no longer the cool boss trading tales. He put up his hands when Hazel fixed him with a glare. "Hey, I'm running a business. I gotta feed my kid."

She slammed her pad on the counter, vaguely aware of it bouncing back to hit the floor as she stomped away to gather the dirty dishes. A litany of muttered curses bubbling under her breath aborted mid-stream.

Best had slotted two twenties under his coffee mug. Beneath them was a paper napkin on which he'd scribbled *Dylan*, followed by a series of digits.

He had left her his phone number.

# Chapter Two

Sadie breezed into the diner well after the lunch hour stampede. She flashed Hazel a lazy smile and pushed her wide, white-rimmed sunglasses into her hair. It might as well have been a summons. Hazel followed her into the back, where Sadie all but stretched out on the narrow bench between their lockers.

"Did you ever notice how good it smells in here?" She filled her lungs with breath. "Think Marco burns incense or something? Man..." Dyed blonde curls brushed the floor as she laced her fingers across her stomach. "It's like peaches or something, right? Maybe pomegranates—"

"Are you *high*?"

"Shh," Sadie giggled. Levering up onto her elbows seemed to take it out of her, because she huffed and puffed with effort. "No, I'm not." A lock of flaxen hair fell into her eyes. She blew it out, grinning. "I, uh... I think I met someone."

Hazel's stomach plummeted, dismay weighing her down. The news wasn't one. Sadie fell in and out of love at least three times a week—usually with prohibitively expensive shoes or Hollywood actors whose pictures she pinned to her Pinterest board. But this time, she'd fallen in love with a flesh and blood man that she'd actually met.

A guy who just so happened to be the standard variety of double-dealing asshole that didn't deserve Sadie.

"Oh, hon..." Hazel stuck a hand into the voluminous pocket of her apron. Dylan Best's phone number crinkled in her grasp.

Sadie pulled her knees up to her chin. "Do you remember Frank?"

Hazel frowned, unclenching her fingers. Had she heard that right?

"Med School Frank?"

Sadie's aunts had taken up the cause of finding her a husband soon after she'd turned eighteen. Eight years later, they were still going strong, undaunted by Sadie's choosy nature. Med School Frank was the latest in a long line of suitors whose accomplishments and pedigree had been first vetted by Sadie's aunts and the other ladies at the hairdresser's where her mother worked.

"He came by last night," Sadie gushed.

"At midnight?"

"Well, no. Earlier. He left flowers and a note." She rummaged in her Louis Vuitton knockoff for the missive. "Aha!" Her smile was triumphant as she plucked out the envelope.

It was, Hazel had to admit, a very nice gesture. Most of Sadie's admirers could barely manage texting—although they were very adept at sending her dick pics.

Sadie hugged her jean-clad calves and propped her chin on a tear in the distressed denim. "He didn't source the poem, but still... What do you think?"

Hazel took her time, considered her response. Sadie gave her heart like some people dispensed bird feed. Inevitably, that meant she often got hurt.

"Byron," Hazel murmured, having scanned the careful, blocky penmanship. "Nice."

"I know, right?" Sadie hitched up her shoulders. "I was thinking I might swing by tonight... His mother's hosting the other biddies for mah jong. He'll be so bored."

It sounded like her mind was already made up, a sign that Hazel's input was expected to flow in the same direction.

*Better Med School Frank than Wall Street Best...*

"What about last night?" Hazel asked as the note exchanged hands again. "You gonna call Tall, Dark and Handsome?"

"Probably not. Why? Do you think I should?"

She had a round, doll-like face, the kind Hazel would've expected to see in cereal commercials on TV. No wonder talent scouts had invited her to a couple of castings when she was a teen. No wonder her mother had refused. Hollywood was a mere stone's throw away, teeming with impressionable young women—a scary prospect for a single mother from the Midwest.

That cautious gene must have skipped a generation. Sadie was as impulsive as she was beautiful.

Hazel's heart bounced against her diaphragm, a cork in water. Trying to steer Sadie away from harm sometimes only encouraged her to cannonball straight into it.

"No... Not if you don't want to."

"Dylan was nice and all, but... Eh." Sadie's scale for acceptable lovers ran from *eh* to *I'm in love*, and she was as likely to take long walks up that spectrum as she was to demote a potential suitor to *what a loser* at a moment's notice. "Frankly, I kind of thought he was more your type." She cocked her head, narrowing her almond brown eyes at Hazel. "You know, nerdy-cute. Did I tell you he wears reading glasses?" She hadn't. "But you swore off guys," Sadie went on, sighing, "so I guess he'll just have to die a bachelor."

"He'll cope."

Marco yelled for them from the front of the diner, their absence noticed at long last.

*Saved by the bellowing boss.* Hazel flashed Sadie a small smile. "Can't wait to start calling you Mrs. Doctor."

"And come play mah jong at my villa!" Sadie's cackle followed Hazel out of the narrow changing room. It wasn't the first time they had camouflaged sour grapes with glee.

\* \* \* \*

Marco had shaken his head when Hazel told him she'd take Sadie's evening shift. "I practically live here," he'd sighed, "but you don't have to."

"You pay me enough." She reasoned that she owed him. If he complained, it was only because he wanted Sadie around. The less he saw of her, the more he wanted her—and the less Hazel could buy that Sadie didn't know what she was doing.

"No, I don't."

Hazel mulled that over as the bus squeaked and rattled down the empty streets. Sadie had borrowed the Volvo. She was counting on coming home late, she said, but Hazel knew that meant she wasn't counting on coming home at all. Hazel pictured her driving up Mulholland with Frank in the passenger seat, his bug eyes blown wide behind thick glasses.

*Don't be mean.* She had glimpsed his picture on Facebook—courtesy of Sadie's religiously upheld post-date debriefings—and he wasn't bad. A little prone to that wide-eyed look of surprise some people wore whenever a camera was pointed at them, but only vaguely Anthony Perkins-ish otherwise.

It didn't hurt that he was Chinese, either. Less chance of a veto from the Ling clan.

The bus lurched to a stop and a couple wearing matching parkas rose from their seats. Hazel covered her mouth with a yawn as she watched them step out. At least she could sleep in tomorrow. She was due for a long, lazy morning. The blisters on her feet alone would welcome the reprieve.

"I like your hair," a voice said over her left shoulder.

Hazel sat up, plastic chair squeaking beneath her. The speaker was a broad-shouldered man wearing a Lakers cap. He smiled when he caught her eye.

"Thanks," Hazel murmured.

Trying to be discreet, she drew her purse closer to her hip.

The man noticed.

"What? You think I'm gonna rob you?" he snorted. The clank and jangle of the bus wasn't loud enough to conceal the sigh of the seat as he tipped forward. "Hey, I asked you a question."

Hazel closed her eyes. Cars flashed past the scuffed window, a rapid succession of lights and shiny paint jobs, like fireflies in the dark. She knew there was no point in rushing for the front of the bus. The driver wouldn't want to get involved. If she got up now, the asshole sitting behind her would become even more enraged.

She wished she hadn't given Sadie the keys with the pepper spray still on the chain.

"C'mon, now," the man said, wheedling. "You ain't doing a very good job of proving those 'dumb blonde' jokes wrong."

Hazel felt him wrap a lock of hair around his finger as the driver braked at the next stop. Revulsion roiled in the pit of her stomach. *Camera flash. "It's just us, baby…"*

She bolted from her seat like a jack-in-the-box, practically leaping through the doors and onto the sidewalk as soon as the doors slid open. Her steps ate up all five hundred feet to her apartment building. She didn't breathe until she could put a couple of locked doors between herself and the outside world.

The prickle in her scalp where the hair had torn loose barely registered.

Mostly, she felt shame. *If Sadie were with you, she would've turned around and given that jerk what for. Why can't you?*

Hazel's cell shrieked into the silence of the apartment. She plucked it out with unsteady fingers. "Mama, hi…"

"Oh, good, I thought you'd be asleep." Her mother took no notice of Hazel's quaking voice.

Hazel frowned at the wood grain of the front door and concentrated on getting her breath back.

"Why are you whispering? What's wrong? Is Dad—?"

"Your father's asleep. Nothing's wrong." A good Southern woman wouldn't admit otherwise under pain of death. Mrs. Whitley was nothing if not a good Southern woman. "You haven't RSVP'd."

"What?" It might have been the adrenaline pumping in Hazel's bloodstream, but though both words and disappointment registered, neither made sense.

"The Facebook event?" Mrs. Whitley sighed. Hazel pictured her pinching the bridge of her nose, winged glasses twitching up and down on her fingertips. "Are you coming to the baby shower?"

*Oh.* Now Hazel remembered. "Probably not..."

"Rhonda was hoping you would."

*But you're relieved I'm not.* Hazel swallowed the retort as she toed off her shoes and stripped out of her denim jacket. "Tell her I can't afford the plane ticket."

"She'd offer to lend you the money. You know what she's like."

Hazel knew. Rhonda was her brother's 'can do no wrong' wife. Class president, preacher's daughter, single-handed organizer of raffles and food drives to help Dunby's indigent population from sinking into delinquency. She was Med School Frank's polar opposite—no matter how impromptu the photo op, she was always camera-ready, her smile as blinding as a fleet of stars.

It was impossible not to envy her. It was also impossible not to feel bad about letting her down.

"Say I have to work," Hazel suggested.

"You could find someone to take your shift, couldn't you?" One question prefaced another before Hazel could get a word in edgewise. "How *is* Sadie Ling?"

*We're doing this again, are we?* Sadie's reputation had never endeared her to many mothers around Dunby, something to do with the Lolita antics she'd supposedly got up to with some of the high school teachers.

All lies and rumors, but the small town gossips didn't care to be set right.

Hazel flopped down onto her futon and glared at the silent television. Unfortunately, the TV didn't cower in response. "Do you *want* me there, Ma?"

Silence on the other end of the line.

"I'll call her to apologize," Hazel promised. "Is that okay?"

"Do it tomorrow," her mother advised. "It's already short notice."

Hazel wondered what her mother would've done if she had said she'd already bought her ticket. It didn't even have to be a flight. She could just take the Greyhound. LA to Missouri wasn't that far. Even Dunby, tucked neatly into the boot of the 'Show Me' state, couldn't quite escape being connected to the rest of the country.

Not for lack of trying.

"You and Dad doing all right?"

"We're fine," Mrs. Whitley replied crisply. "Buddy comes by every Sunday." *And you don't.* It went without saying.

"He does have the advantage of living right next door."

"Next door are the Rileys. Buddy moved into the Gainses' colonial on Three Lane. I don't know *why* he didn't just demolish that monstrosity and start fresh. There's so much work—"

Hazel pressed a knuckle into her eye socket. "Ma, do you mind if I let you go? I just got off work." The last thing she was in the mood for was a retrospective of her brother's domestic arrangements.

*I'm living in a shoebox apartment and struggling to make rent. Thanks for asking.*

Her mother's reply was icy, affronted. It was rude to interrupt. "Don't forget Rhonda."

"I won't." *How could I, when I have you to remind me?* "'Night, Ma..." The line went dead before the words were fully out of her mouth. Hazel dropped the cell onto the couch and tipped her head against the backrest. "Love you, too," she murmured, to no one in particular.

* * * *

The gap-toothed toddler gazing up at her from his mother's arms made it virtually impossible not to smile. "All right, two Sloppy Joes coming up—hey!"

Breath left Hazel's lungs in a rush.

Sadie's hold on her elbow was punishing, but it was the tense expression on her face that stunned Hazel.

"We'll be right back," Sadie told their bewildered clients with a tepid smile.

She left Hazel with a choice between walking and being dragged away over the sticky linoleum. Hazel spurred her feet. Sadie seemed resolute enough to use force.

"Okay, *what?*"

Sadie knew all about the no-touching policy—every painful, humiliating detail—so whatever had her breaking the holiest commandment must have been big.

"He's here," Sadie hissed between clenched teeth, once they were safely inside the kitchen doorway.

"George Clooney?"

Through a billowing cloud of steam, Sadie glowered.

"Jesus?" Hazel guessed, throwing up her hands. "I got nothing."

"*Dylan.*"

A cold shiver rippled down Hazel's spine. She didn't have to play the 'Dylan, who?' charade because one glance at the door confirmed it. Best wasn't alone this time. Three other men were with him, laughing and talking in too-loud voices as they scrutinized the diner for a free table.

"You have to take 'em," Sadie entreated.

"I do?"

"I didn't *call*."

Hazel sighed. "Keep tallying up the IOUs and you're gonna end up having to murder someone for me just to even up the score." She picked out four greasy menus. "You bus the corner booth in my section real quick."

Sadie bolted like the Energizer bunny.

"Gentlemen," Hazel greeted, frosty smile in place. "Welcome to The Last Crab Pub. How many?"

Dylan turned to face her, eyebrows climbing half an inch up his brow. He was wearing a suit again—ash gray—with a baby-blue tie. He even wore a pocket square. It wouldn't have surprised Hazel to discover that each individual strand of his shiny raven hair had been painstakingly arranged with tweezers before being gelled in place.

She wished it left her cold.

"The Last what?" one of his friends snorted. "Menu reads *Marco's…*"

"Does it?" Hazel feigned surprise. From the corner of her eye, she glimpsed Sadie making her way out of her section with a thumbs-up. "Huh. How about that? Let me show you to your table."

Dylan's friends fell into step behind her like ducklings in a row.

"So does that mean you serve seafood?" asked the pedant of the group.

"No."

Hazel stood idly by while they crammed themselves into the vinyl booth. At least two of the men seemed perplexed by their surroundings. Dylan wasn't among them. The intensity of his stare was beginning to render Hazel uncomfortable, but she couldn't very well throw him out—or, worse, go to Marco and ask *him* to do the throwing out. He didn't usually like to interfere until and unless a client took creepiness to the point of groping.

She wasn't going to risk her job for the likes of Dylan Best.

"No," Hazel repeated, clearing her throat, "but the pork chops are pretty good. I'll let you look over the menu." She couldn't get away fast enough.

"So?" Sadie murmured as they convened behind the bar under the guise of passing orders back and forth to the kitchen. "What did he say?"

"He's totally heartbroken. Hasn't slept a day in five weeks."

Sadie gave her a playful shove. "You're the worst. I almost started feeling bad for the guy."

"You must not have seen his Rolex."

"I'll make it up to you," Sadie promised before sauntering away with a tray filled with sweet potato hash, tamales and French fries.

Out of curiosity, Hazel slanted a glance to Dylan's table. She wasn't surprised to find his dark gaze didn't track Sadie across the diner, but she didn't know what to do with their eyes locking across the room.

Dylan cut his eyes away first. It didn't help.

He was perfectly cordial when Hazel went to retrieve their drinks order. The rest of his buddies likewise kept to themselves. They went quiet whenever Hazel returned to their table, as though whatever it was they were discussing was too important to let strangers overhear.

It was a relief to drop off their check an hour later. Whenever she turned back to the room, she couldn't shake the sense that someone was watching her — and that said someone was Dylan.

She jumped when she heard him clear his throat from the other side of the counter.

"Do you take credit cards?" he asked, holding up the check.

"Yeah..." *You couldn't wait until I came back to your table to ask?* Hazel rolled her tongue against the roof of her mouth. She'd made it this far without causing a scene, she could go a little further.

Dylan slid his leather wallet out of his coat. Hazel suspected it probably cost as much as her rent. It even smelled new.

She glanced away as she waited for him to hand over his Visa.

"Did you have a good time?"

Marco insisted on friendliness. *Clients want to feel special. That's why they come here instead of the Olive Garden across the street. It's all about the dining experience.*

Hazel often wondered if he'd swallowed a marketing course book.

"Yes, it was great," Dylan replied, too kneejerk to be sincere.

Hazel aimed her smile at the cash register. "Your buddies are like fish out of water."

"It's their first time out of Century City."

"Ouch. Culture shock," Hazel drawled. She knew where she stood with the Brentwood types — easily recognized outside their leafy green territory by the faint sneers they all wore when exposed to the common folk—but Century City mostly kept to itself. It was busy enough that its residents never really needed to venture out, except perhaps into equally hectic Beverly Hills.

They certainly never traveled as far as Marco's for the sake of a burger. Dylan must have deliberately taken them out of their natural habitat. And he had brought them here, to the hole in the wall where Sadie worked.

"You're not from around here either, are you?" Dylan ventured.

"No."

"Me neither."

"You blend in well," Hazel countered. "I look at your foursome and I can barely tell the difference."

Dylan winced and pressed a hand to his chest. "That bad?" He took his credit card back with a headshake. "Then I suppose there's no point asking if you'd like to have coffee sometime."

"I don't drink coffee." *Wait, what?*

No one was more surprised than Hazel at the answer, but Dylan's jaw actually seemed to go a little slack, like he couldn't believe she hadn't shot him down.

"Okay... Tea?"

"In California?"

"Water?" Dylan guessed. "Or—would you have dinner with me?"

*No way.* Sadie was shooting her wary glances from across the room, probably wondering if she should interject. Other patrons were waiting for their orders, their checks. Urgency slithered under Hazel's skin, throbbing like a headache.

"Yeah, okay," she heard herself reply. It was a strange, almost out of body experience, watching astonishment morph into pleasure on Dylan's lips.

"Tomorrow night?"

Hazel grimaced. "I have to work... Monday? My shift ends at six." She wanted nothing more than to excise that finagling, apologetic note in her voice.

Why was she trying to accommodate him? She couldn't be considering this with any real degree of interest. *Agreeing to dinner isn't the same as going.* Dylan wouldn't be the first guy she had stood up.

*Going to dinner isn't the same as sleeping with him.* Her track record over the past three years begged to differ.

"You done?" asked one of Dylan's buddies, clamping a hand onto his shoulder.

He straightened. "Yes. Thank you," he added, speaking strictly to Hazel.

"Hope to see you back soon." She couldn't believe the words had come out of her mouth until he was out of the diner, one with the evening gloom.

Sadie materialized at her elbow. "What did he want?"

"To ask me out." It didn't occur to Hazel to lie.

"Wow... What a creep."

"Thanks," Hazel scoffed.

Sadie smacked her lips. "That's not what I meant... He didn't even say hi to me. And now he's asking you out, knowing I'm watching?" Sadie clucked her tongue. "Dick move."

*Of course, why else would he do it?*

"Yeah." Maybe Sadie was right. Maybe there was nothing more to Dylan's offer than an attempt to punish Sadie. He wouldn't be the first jerk who liked to slap a woman around in bed and meddle in her life outside of it. Hazel had time to figure it out until Monday night.

She was probably going to cancel.

# Chapter Three

Hazel had been going to cancel. She had his number. She could have done it by text — pretend something came up and avoid what was sure to be an uncomfortable evening with a man who wasn't even interested in her.

She hadn't done it Sunday night because *Fried Green Tomatoes* had been on. She hadn't done it Monday morning because she'd had just an hour before work to go to the gym and ignore the leering meatheads. By Monday at lunch, it had seemed like short notice, which was why that evening at six o'clock, she found herself leaving the diner with Dylan beside her.

Sadie caught her eye on the way out and pursed her lips. They hadn't talked about the offer since Saturday. She must have thought the matter settled.

"So, where do you want to go?" Dylan asked and opened the passenger door to a silver Tesla. "I imagine you must be sick of diners by now —"

"Do you cook?" Hazel cut in.

He hesitated. "Sort of?"

"Farmer's market is on the way." *If you can't beat 'em, make them as uncomfortable as you can.* "We can grab a few things. I'll make a casserole." If growing up in the Midwest had taught Hazel anything, it was never to underestimate the emotional balm of a hearty, cheese-filled dish.

Dylan pushed past bemusement with a shrug. "Farmer's market it is." He slid so elegantly behind the wheel that the leather seats didn't dare squeak.

As soon as he powered the engine, a warble of electric guitar and earworm drumming filled the inside of the sleek interior of the car. Dylan wasn't quick enough to dim the volume before Hazel recognized the singer.

"You listen to Momo Wu?"

"You know c-pop?" Dylan arched an eyebrow.

Hazel shrugged. "Some. It's Sadie's way of keeping in touch with her roots." *What's your excuse?*

"Oh, I hadn't realized."

"Really." It was Hazel's turn to let disbelief flash across her face. Despite the dyed blonde hair, Sadie made no secrets of her origins. She'd gone through a phase back in college when she had decked herself out in cheongsams and paper fans. It might have been a cry for attention. Hazel couldn't say.

She had been too busy crying for herself back then.

Dylan prudently joined the flow of traffic. "I don't mean... She didn't mention I'm studying Mandarin?" He chanced a glance at Hazel, who merely pressed her lips into a thin line.

Of course Dylan would assume they had spent hours conferring about his quirks. Pop culture agreed that overthinking was an intrinsic female trait.

"There's a chance I might be moving to Shanghai," he added by way of explanation. "The whole connecting with your roots thing... I'm trying that, too. And audio books only get me so far."

It was too earnest to be easily dismissed. Hazel nearly regretted her quick tongue. "So you're bridging the gap with Chinese pop music?"

"I almost have *Lady First* memorized," Dylan boasted.

"For its musical virtues or the knee sock-wearing songstresses?" Hazel bit the inside of her cheek. "You know, that calls for a demonstration..."

Dylan's grin dug dimples into his clean-shaven cheeks. "Maybe after dinner."

"I'll hold you to that," Hazel added weakly, trying to hold back a smirk. *So much for putting him on the spot.* Dylan seemed to be up to the challenge. How c-pop karaoke fit with the rich and powerful alpha male shtick, she couldn't say, but experience confirmed that no Dominant was all whips and chains all the time.

Sometimes they dabbled in flash photography, as well.

Hazel turned her head so Dylan wouldn't catch her biting her lip and squeezing her eyes shut.

They made a quick stop at the market. On Hazel's orders, Dylan remained in the car while she availed herself of fresh produce. She got fennel, broccoli and cauliflower, plus a couple of tomatoes for color. Not knowing if Dylan had any bacon in the house, she bought that, too, as well as an indispensable block of cheddar. Dylan grinned through the windshield when he saw her return with arms laden.

"This looks promising," he said, rushing to help her with the bags. "Are we feeding a regiment?"

"You'll be eating like one when I'm done with you." It almost sounded like flirting, but since Hazel seldom did that anymore, she couldn't be sure it qualified.

"Promises, promises," Dylan sighed, but that delighted grin didn't leave his lips until they had made their way to his apartment. There it flickered and died abruptly, his face falling as he cut off the engine. He made no move to pull the key from the ignition. He was staring fixedly at the BMW parked outside four-seven-one Aulden Way as though the hood emblem offended him.

"Is...everything okay?" Hazel asked, old fears surfacing like oil in water.

"Yeah, it's just..." Dylan frowned. "I was counting on telling you this over dinner..."

"You're married."

"What? No—"

"You have a girlfriend and that's her car?" Somehow, Hazel successfully kept her voice from shaking. She felt calm, if a little disappointed. It wasn't as though she hadn't received ample warning to stay away from Dylan Best. The universe could only do so much to make her pay attention.

He shook his head. "Not a girlfriend. Not anything, really... I don't live alone. My, uh, roommate and I have an arrangement."

His gaze was soft when he met Hazel's eyes, pleading with her to understand. She rolled her eyes. "If it makes her uncomfortable when you bring girls home, I think you both need a reality check."

"It's not a 'her'," Dylan replied tersely. Hazel couldn't pretend his firm rebuke didn't send a zing through her body. "Nor is it a matter of discomfort." His expression shifted in and out of distress as he squeezed the steering wheel. "I'm sorry. We could have dinner somewhere else. I know a few good restaurants."

"Or we could go to my place." Clearly the filter between Hazel's brain and her mouth was in a state of disrepair. *Either that or Mama was right all along – pop music really does rot your brain.* "I mean," she hastened to add, "we could totally call it a night, but…"

"Won't that be weird, with Sadie there?"

Hazel frowned, puzzled. "Why would Sadie be in my apartment?" Again that stubborn ache roiled in the pit of Hazel's stomach. "Did you…? Did you want her to be there?"

The suspicion that Dylan was angling for some sort of three-way romp surged to the forefront of her thoughts once again. It had served as reassurance the first time they met – if Dylan was just another randy hog, then Hazel didn't need to examine the butterflies in her belly or consider that she might be attracted to her friend's one-night stand.

"I thought you guys lived together," he said, shaking his head.

*That's not an answer.* "We don't," Hazel retorted curtly. She didn't want to dig any deeper.

Dylan smiled. "Oh. Okay. Then sure, yeah. Let's have dinner at your place."

When Hazel offered no further protest, they peeled away from the curb with a squeal of tires, leaving four-seven-one Aulden and its conspicuous BMW in the dust.

* * * *

Hazel's apartment was one of four units on the sixth floor of a nondescript building in the southernmost tip of South Los Angeles. They were, technically, not quite part of the city, not really considered 'the suburbs'. Accordingly, rent was affordable and the amenities in her area left much to be desired. The potholed streets tested the Tesla's suspensions as Hazel played GPS.

"I know it doesn't look it, but it's pretty safe," she ventured.

"I'm not worried," Dylan said, but the narrowed-eyed gaze he directed at his surroundings belied that sentiment.

He insisted on helping Hazel with the groceries, which meant that she had no choice but to brave the stairs empty-handed. To fill the silence, she found herself calling attention to every snag in their path the way a tour guide would be pointing out landmarks in Hollywood. *And on your right, behold a suspicious yellow stain. Mind you, don't step in it with your expensive Italian shoes!*

The elevator was once again out of order.

It was a relief to unlatch her apartment door and lead the way inside. Hazel gulped down a couple of breaths, her pulse thumping in her ears. "Put the bags down wherever..." The entryway led directly into the living room, which itself led into the bedroom. The kitchen lay to the left of the front door, as narrow as it was dark.

Dylan picked the chipped counter to deposit the groceries, pushing a couple of boxes of cereal aside to make room. If he noticed the decrepit cupboards or the paint peeling from the window frames, he didn't let on. Concern twisted at his features when he turned back to heaving, panting Hazel. "You all right?"

"I hate taking the stairs."

"But it's so good for you," Dylan needled. "Like broccoli." His grin seemed taxing somehow, like he was struggling to play the joker though he didn't feel up to the part.

He seemed to be waiting for Hazel to grill him about the roommate. She couldn't pretend she didn't feel a little tempted. *None of my business.* The longer it stayed that way, the better. Curiosity was a two-way street.

"Okay. Cheese casserole. I know you said you don't cook, but if I give you a knife and tell you to chop things, we won't end up in the ER, right?"

Dylan smirked. "I said I *sort of* cook. More precisely, I'm an expert slicer and dicer." He slowly peeled off his jacket and hung it from the back of an armchair, fastidiously brushing away an imaginary bit of lint.

Even as she watched him roll up his sleeves, Hazel had a hard time picturing Dylan in shorts and cotton tee. His 'look' was so painstakingly put together that she felt like a reject from the nineties by comparison. At least she'd thought to iron-curl her hair this morning. Some of the whorls still held out after a day's work, bouncing on her shoulders as she unloaded the vegetables and got the oven running.

Between the two of them, they assembled the ingredients quickly. Dylan took direction like he did everything else—gracefully, with a nod of thanks when Hazel corrected him. She tried not to get too bogged down in tweaking the way he held the knife or the size of the florets carved.

*No one likes a nag,* as her last boyfriend would say.

"So… Did Sadie tell you we lived together?" Hazel asked, sliding the casserole into the oven.

"No. Now that I think of it, she didn't." Dylan tucked his hands into his pockets and shrugged. He cut a distracting picture, holding up the doorframe with his shoulder. "I must have inferred."

"Is it weird that I live alone?"

"It's…convenient." He smiled with half a mouth.

"Sometimes," Hazel agreed. She'd finished wiping her hands dry on the dishcloth, but couldn't remember what to do with it after that. "Occasionally it also means that I forget to buy basic necessities, like wine or beer... I have some iced tea, if you want. Or gin?" She could practically hear her mother tut-tutting from eighteen hundred miles away.

"Why not both?"

It was that flash of genius that had them retiring to the couch with a half-empty bottle of Seagram's Extra Dry and two cans of iced tea, grimacing in unison as they tasted the blend.

"Oh my God," Hazel choked out, "that's foul."

Dylan gagged discreetly. Then he burst out laughing. "This might be the worst thing I've ever tasted." He took another sip as if to check and coughed. "Yep, it's confirmed."

"I'd apologize, but it *was* your idea..."

"Just goes to show," Dylan said sagely.

"What?"

"Never trust a financial analyst." He raised his glass in mock toast and took another pouting sip.

"Huh. I had you pegged for a banker — or a Silicon Valley lawyer." Firms had sprung up like mushrooms after rain since formerly hip companies started hopping onto the stock market train.

"Oh, that explains why you always look so pleased to see me!" Dylan laughed.

"Maybe I just don't like your face."

"Bullshit. I've got a very pretty face. I'm like a Chinese George Clooney." He smiled at Hazel over the coffee table. He'd claimed the armchair while she took the futon, an equitable division of furniture that kept Hazel from feeling too boxed in. "*Is* that the reason?"

If they weren't going to talk about his mysterious roommate, maybe it was only normal that they'd talk about her not so mysterious friend.

Hazel rolled her shoulders against the backrest. "To be honest, I wasn't super excited to see the guy who sleeps with one woman and gives his number to another..." It didn't explain why she'd agreed to have dinner with him instead of refusing—noisily and on the spot. There were limits to good manners.

Dylan scowled. The way he did it, though, was less menacing and more a means of spelling out his bewilderment. Hazel wondered if he practiced in the mirror. She couldn't be the only one calibrating her smiles so they didn't seem too inviting, too open or keeping her scowls from offending people who could hurt her.

"I...didn't give you my number because I was trying to pick you up. It was meant for Sadie. In case..." Dylan waved the hand that held his glass in a wide arc. "I don't know. She swore she was fine, but I still spent that night thinking that I should have insisted she stay over—to make sure."

"Aftercare." Hazel didn't realize she'd spoken aloud until she saw Dylan nod.

"Precisely."

The revelation should have made her feel relieved that Dylan put so much thought into what he did. Her memory snagged on another detail. "That's why you wanted me to come in?"

"Ninety percent of the why."

Their eyes met and locked fast. Hazel felt a surge of heat eddying up from her core all the way to the tips of her fingers. If it stained her cheeks pink along the way, she wouldn't have been surprised.

"Do you do that—what you did with Sadie... Do you do it with many women?"

"Are you asking if I'm a man whore?" Dylan sucked his lips into his mouth as though he was struggling not to smile.

"Hey, if the safe word fits..."

He chuckled. "I don't. I have a few female friends who share my interests and we see each other from time to time. Sadie was a rare exception." Dylan peered into his glass and compressed his lips into a rueful smile. "I probably shouldn't ask, but..."

"No," Hazel interjected. "She didn't say why she didn't call." More and more, Dylan seemed like he should have been her type—wealthy, educated, *very* handsome. And he was into the same kinks as Sadie.

The aunties would be bowled over if they heard he was actively trying to renew his ties to the old country.

Hazel could have left it at that. She could have extricated herself from the topic without giving Dylan extra ammunition. But a part of her was beginning to feel like this wasn't war and she didn't have to worry about buttressing her defenses. She knew what it was like on Dylan's side of the equation far more than she understood Sadie's. She empathized.

"If I had to guess, I'd say it's less to do with you than her," Hazel opined evenly. "Sadie's looking for *the one*." The air-quotes were an imperative.

"And I wasn't it."

Hazel hid her headshake behind her glass. The iced tea and gin cocktail was absolutely foul, but if it chased away the panicky tremors, then it was good enough.

"Well," Dylan said, "here's hoping it was nothing more serious."

"Like what?" Hazel tasted rubber in the back of her mouth. A white flash ignited before her eyes, setting off brightly colored fireworks. Somewhere, a man patted her hip and told her she was beautiful.

Dylan's voice pulled her back into the present. "I don't want to shock you."

*How sweet.* "Go ahead, if you want. Sadie keeps me informed." Mostly because they swam in the same murky waters—Sadie merely chased her cravings with abandon, while Hazel embraced celibacy. Neither of them needed Dylan protecting their virgin ears.

To his credit, he didn't waste time hemming and hawing. "To put it delicately, I'm always wary of taking a new partner. I'm never entirely sure they know what they're getting into. Your friend wouldn't be the first submissive I've had who panicked after a session."

And, just like that, Hazel's ears were ringing, *submissive* ricocheting like a stray bullet in the hollow recesses of her skull. "What about *during*?"

"That, too." Dylan tipped forward in his seat, resting his elbows on his knees. "I'm sorry. If this is making you uncomfortable—"

"It's not," Hazel lied, as abrupt as a bee sting.

"You look like you're about to break that glass."

Hazel glanced down at her hands. Her knuckles had indeed gone white with tension. She hadn't even noticed.

She hurried to release it, gin and iced tea sloshing against the sides of the glass as Hazel set it on the coffee table. "I should check on dinner."

Providentially, Dylan didn't give chase. He was still seated, still staring contemplatively into his glass when Hazel returned with two plated slices of gooey cheese casserole.

"Oh, that smells *good*," he purred.

"Careful, it's hot."

"Words to live by," Dylan quipped. They didn't stop him trying a forkful of still steaming casserole, then dousing his scalded tongue in spiked iced tea.

Hazel couldn't help a chuckle. "I did warn you..."

"Yeah, but the forbidden is *always* more attractive. It's Biblical."

"Not sure that was the point of that particular story, but I won't debate you. My Sunday school days are long behind me."

"That's still more than I know." Dylan grinned and tapped his chest. "Jewish, I'm afraid."

Sadie's aunts wouldn't have thought much of *that*. By that same token, neither would Hazel's mother.

"I'm guessing *not* Orthodox..."

"What gave it away? The eyes or—"

"The string of ex-girlfriends you like to tie up and torture with a feather," Hazel deadpanned, before blowing lightly on a forkful of casserole.

Dylan gaped. "Now that's just deliberately misrepresenting reality."

"No feathers?"

"No ex-girlfriends."

"Why?" It wasn't an absurd question. As far as Hazel could tell, Dylan was funny and charming, he drove a nice car and he had a well-paying job. The roommate thing was obviously a sticking point, but women would put up with a lot more for a boyfriend who treated them well.

Hazel wasn't sure if she counted herself among them, ancient history notwithstanding.

She watched Dylan's expression shift as though he was picking his way through several possible answers. In the end, he settled on a shrug. "I'm not really looking for a partner."

"But you'll toss and turn all night long for a stranger you happen to sleep with?"

She couldn't say why she felt compelled to needle him. She just did.

"That's half of the reason why I usually *don't* sleep with strangers," Dylan retorted.

"What's the other half?"

It was Dylan's turn to deadpan. "I'm sleeping with my roommate."

Hazel opened her mouth, realized she had nothing to say and closed it again. Her gin-soaked brain took a moment to process his reply. Dylan's 'it's complicated' romantic entanglements were shaping up to sound like something out of *Days of Our Lives*.

"So you're…"

"Bisexual," Dylan finished for her. "And sort of involved with someone, yes… If you want me to leave, I can show myself out."

The offer carried some weight, if only because some people had hidden depths and others had goddamn Mariana trenches. Hazel mulled it over.

She shook her head.

# Chapter Four

After dinner, Dylan insisted on doing the dishes. "It's only fair," he said, once again rolling up his sleeves. "You cooked. I'm in charge of clean-up."

"And what am I supposed to do?" Hazel wanted to know.

He shrugged. "The possibilities are endless." He wouldn't be put off his stride, so Hazel threw up her hands in resignation and allowed him to get on with it.

The kitchen was too small to fit a dishwasher, so Dylan had to scrub the plates by hand. He ran the water hot enough that eddies of steam rose up from the sink and clung to the windowpane like tears. After a beat, they dribbled down—also very much like tears.

Hazel hopped up onto the counter, a fresh glass of ice tea and gin in hand. The cocktail improved on acquaintance. She spared a thought for the rotting pulped wood beneath her, hoping against hope that it wouldn't give out under her sizable thighs. Her landlord would be furious, for one thing, and she didn't want to become Dylan's 'fat girl anecdote,' for another.

She drowned the notion in gin.

She couldn't say when she had started caring what exactly she might be to Dylan, but it was a recent development. Not being revolted by his mere existence had snuck up on her. It was a short journey from there to admiring the slope of Dylan's shoulders or the hum of his voice as he sponged off the remaining flakes of dried cheese still stubbornly glued to their plates.

"Does Sadie know?"

"That my true calling is washing dishes?" Dylan retorted, flashing her a shit-eating grin.

"No... That you're not completely single." The nuance seemed to matter to Dylan. Hazel thought he was lying to himself. Either he was in a relationship or he wasn't. Either he was cheating on his partner — his *male* partner — or he wasn't.

Dylan embraced the silence for a long beat. Only the clink of knives and forks in the drying rack disturbed the quiet. He shut off the tap. "We didn't discuss that, no. I was under the impression that my situation was irrelevant to Sadie."

When he felt cornered, Dylan's voice seemed to drop an octave. His speech patterns went all Ivy League. He also pulled back his shoulders, like he was facing down a fashion runway — or a challenger in the boxing ring. Hazel tried not to examine his tell too closely. Reading people was a double-edged sword. Sometimes they wound up returning the favor.

"What about your other lady-friends?" she pressed. "Do they know?"

"Yes."

"They don't care?"

Dylan turned to face her, dishcloth hanging from his hands like a slightly soiled white flag. "Why should they? I've never offered to be anyone's boyfriend. Some of them are married. It's just that their needs and mine occasionally dovetail, so we meet up."

"And your…partner doesn't feel cheated?"

"No." Dylan's smile didn't reach his eyes. He helped himself to what was left of his third glass, downing the contents in one gulp. "You must think we're perverts. First the S&M, now this…"

"Does it matter what I think?" Hazel asked, because the former had long ago stopped making her uneasy. As far as she could tell, Dylan had a working arrangement with his partner—she kept wanting to call him *boyfriend*—and he got his rocks off consensually with like-minded women.

The opinion of a diner waitress who barely made minimum wage wasn't worth much.

"I wouldn't be here and I wouldn't have told you about my situation if I didn't care."

Dylan's reply curbed the joke that perched on Hazel's lips, shooting it down before it could be uttered. He sounded so genuine. And Hazel—well, maybe she wanted to believe. She set the dregs of her cocktail aside and hooked a hand in his shirtfront.

"I don't know how I feel about all this."

"I can understand that," Dylan hastened to say. "Don't feel there's any pressure to go along with something you don't want or—"

His objections floundered when Hazel pressed her lips to his. Dylan slotted neatly into the V of Hazel's splayed legs, brushing his hands up her thighs as if to confirm that she was, in fact, real.

Hazel nipped idly at his lips, grinning despite herself.

"What's funny?" Dylan asked, his breath gusting against her mouth.

"This is not how I thought tonight would go."

"Oh?"

"I was going to stand you up," Hazel confessed. "Then was I going to be a terrible date so you would stay away from the diner... Where did I go wrong?"

Dylan kissed the lament from her lips, silencing all others before they could bubble out. He was a ridiculously good kisser. He didn't have to grope at Hazel's breasts or try to lift up her shirt to elicit a moan. If anything, she found herself wishing he would up the stakes. But just as she started to wrench his shirt-tails out of his pants, Dylan pulled back.

"What?" Hazel breathed. Her throat was dry with want. "Did I do something wrong?"

"No. Not in the least. But we've been drinking and—"

Hazel dropped her hands to the counter with a dull thump. "You've got something against a little liquid courage?"

"I prefer my partners sober," Dylan replied. The deepening furrow between his eyebrows told her he wasn't screwing around.

"Great."

"I had a wonderful time..."

Hazel rolled her eyes and hopped off the counter. She didn't need to nudge Dylan out of the way. He moved willingly. Only the sound of her name on his— talented, wicked—tongue stopped her from walking out of the kitchen and possibly opening the door so he could take off.

"Did you expect me to put out because you treated me to dinner?" The snappish edge in his voice cast some doubt on whether or not he was kidding.

"No," Hazel lied, folding her arms across her small breasts. She hated the way her nipples poked into her shirt. She hated that Dylan could crank her engine with a simple kiss. "And I'm sure you wanted to go out with me because we have such stimulating conversation... Look, it's fine. I just need a little space."

"You and me both," Dylan agreed, leaning against the counter. His gaze was mild, the threadbare hint of a smile flickering into being on his lips. "How are you still single?"

"That doesn't sound like a compliment."

"It's meant to be." Dylan raked a hand through his hair. "You're smart. You're witty... You're very beautiful."

"Easy, Romeo. If you're not going to sleep with me, you don't need to seduce me." Which wasn't to say she didn't enjoy the laundry list of unearned flattery. The kitchen was too narrow for this kind of talk. Hazel picked a breadcrumb off the counter and hurled it into the sink bowl. "I guess I'm not really in the market for a relationship. I'll leave the hunt for true love to Sadie."

"That's good to know."

Hazel hauled a glance his way, grinning when she noticed him doing the same. "Okay, we need to find something else to do before I renege on my promise and jump you where you stand."

"I'm an excellent Monopoly player."

Laughter simmered in Hazel's throat, rising like soap bubbles.

"I'm serious."

Hazel bit her lower lip, but the knot of tension in her belly had come undone and she couldn't seem to will away the inexplicable sense of euphoria. *Must be the booze.* "You know, this is the weirdest date I've ever been on..."

"It's a little strange for me, too," Dylan admitted.

"I don't have a Monopoly board."

"Chess?"

Hazel shook her head.

"Poker?"

"Strip poker," she countered and that *was* the liquor talking, but Dylan didn't back down from the bid.

It was how they found themselves crammed together on her narrow futon, trading grins over the upper edge of their cards. Dylan insisted on Texas Hold'em and Hazel, having no particular preference, went along with it.

She lost the first hand, and consequently her tights. Gin kept her from feeling more than a flicker of mortification for baring chipped, sparkly blue nail polish to Dylan's gaze.

"My turn to deal," she said, wriggling her fingers toward the deck.

"You're not implying I cheat..."

"No, I'm sure you'd *never*."

Dylan smirked as he parted with the deck, their hands brushing in the exchange. "Good job pretending you're not judging me."

"I'm not." Her heated cheeks told a different story.

"Not even a little bit?" Dylan leaned his head against the backrest of the couch, eyes so dark they were nearly all pupil. They told Hazel this was no longer about poker. "It's okay. I'd probably judge me, too."

Self-deprecation always rubbed her the wrong way, but Dylan made it sound genuine. Hazel pursed her lips. "You're a grown man. The way you live your life is none of my business." Not least because this wasn't a date, it was a hook-up, albeit without any hooking up being done because according to Dylan they were both too drunk to consent. Hazel dealt another hand. "Our current pastime aside, I'm sure you're mature enough to know what you're doing."

"I object. Poker is *very* mature."

"Really?" Hazel poked her tongue into her cheek. "Because this brings back memories of college."

Dylan's eyes gleamed when he smiled. "Is that a bad thing? I liked college. Would that I could go back!"

"Easy there, granddad."

"I feel old," he confessed with a counterfeit sigh. "Thirty-three is the new forty, right? I'm sure I read that somewhere."

Hazel scoffed. "Not when you're making six figures a year." Bitter about the cards she'd been dealt? Never.

"Five," Dylan corrected, in a small voice.

"Really?" She wrinkled her lips. "Way to squander that hard-bought Yale education. I bet your Century City friends never let you join in any reindeer games."

"I didn't go to Yale."

"Harvard?" Hazel ventured. He was too Ivy League not to be an alumnus.

Dylan shook his head and studied his cards. "Ledwich U."

"Never heard of it."

"Private college. Very small. It's got maybe about three hundred students? Something like that... All guys."

"Ah, I see. America's last bastion of macho academic sovereignty," Hazel ribbed as she glanced down at her hand. "Is that where you met the roommate?"

On the edge of her peripheral vision, a shadow flitted across Dylan's features. Hazel instantly regretted asking.

"Sorry. It's none of my business..." She couldn't blame it on the gin, either, because she would've been curious anyway. Guilt bit at her insides like a snapping dog. "We don't have to talk." *About that. About anything.* She understood wanting to avoid hot-button issues. "We can just...play cards. I did say you didn't like me for my stimulating conversation." The corners of her lips threatened a smile. She hated herself for the stubborn urge to please.

She hated herself even more for the flash of relief when Dylan curled his fingers around her ankle, something magnanimous and kind in the caress.

He flicked up a glance, expression soft and open. "You're wrong." He won the next hand and smiled beatifically when Hazel peeled off her shirt and threw it at him. "Had enough yet?"

A stubborn Hazel shook her head. She gathered up the cards again.

* * * *

The spill of sunlight through the blinds teased at Hazel's eyelids until she could stand it no more. She rolled over with a groan, turning her face into the pillow in an attempt to get back to sleep.

She was vaguely aware of her legs being bare beneath the covers. *That's weird.* Why wasn't she wearing her PJ bottoms? She remembered Dylan, the hastily assembled supper. She recalled the poker game and her luckless string of consecutive losses.

*Strip poker.*

Hazel bolted upright in bed, heart leaping into her throat.

The right side of the mattress was empty, no dent in the pillow to suggest that a body had lain there. The apartment did not smell like freshly brewed coffee *or* sex. It didn't echo with the prickly, out-of-focus mental snapshots of a drunken fling.

It took Hazel a moment to recall walking Dylan to the door, then peering out of the kitchen window, in the dark, to watch as he boarded his cab five flights below.

Dylan hadn't spent the night. They hadn't done anything worth regretting.

She was about to sink back into the rumpled bedding, relieved, when the doorbell went off.

"It's me!" Sadie shouted into the intercom once Hazel had shambled her way to the door. "Buzz me in, it's freezing out here."

Hazel cast about the room for any signs of compromising activity. Finding none, she did as she was told. She spent the minutes it took Sadie to navigate six flights of stairs pulling on her pajama pants and finger-combing her hair into place. She didn't know why she bothered.

One glance was all it took for Sadie to beam a knowing smile.

"Looks like someone had a rough night!" Sadie breezed into the apartment with a foursome of Starbucks coffees in a disposable carry tray. "Latte, another latte... That's a caramel macchiato—and a frappuccino for me," she rattled off, then plucked out the last and parked herself on Hazel's futon like her presence was a foregone conclusion.

Hazel watched her peel off the plastic lid from her drink and lick the straw.

"So?"

"What?" Hazel took the armchair, trying not to imagine that she could feel Dylan's body heat still somehow clinging to the upholstery. "He's not here."

"You didn't let him spend the night?" Sadie grinned. "You go, girl. Although I think I saw his car parked out front... You sure he's not hiding in the bushes somewhere?"

"Positive." Hazel rolled her eyes. "We didn't fuck."

"Oh." The revelation seemed to take the wind out of Sadie's sails, if only for a moment. "Why not? He do something to piss you off?"

"No."

"You're not into him?"

That would've made it easier. If she could have just brushed last night off as another near-miss, she could put the thought of Dylan Best out of her mind and get back to the regularly scheduled routine of work, home, work, home. "No," Hazel admitted. "It's...complicated." She winced at the words coming out of her mouth. "Christ, I sound like a status update."

"A bit," Sadie confirmed, "but, hey, at least he's not a creep, right? I'm all for not sleeping with a guy on a first date. Cheers." They clinked their Starbucks coffees.

"Thanks. And thanks for the coffee. I know you don't splurge for any occasion." Even with tips, they didn't exactly make bank serving burgers at Marco's. Starbucks was a rainy day extravaganza. It tasted like birthday cake or Christmas.

Hell, it tasted like every breakup Sadie couldn't get over.

Sadie grinned over the rim of her plastic cup. "It's not every day my girl finds a guy worthy of a second look, is it?"

There was nothing in Sadie's expression to suggest that she felt any way other than supportive, but Hazel still wondered. "Is this weird for you? I mean...because it's Dylan." *Because you two had a thing, however brief, and now I'm not doing the sane thing and telling him to get lost.*

"Is it weird for *you*?" Sadie asked.

"Putting those Psych 101 classes to good work, I see..."

The joke fell flat. Sadie didn't so much as crack a smile.

Hazel rallied. "A bit. Knowing right off the bat that he's into...you know. It's something to get used to." The men she'd dated since college were a varied bunch, but they had one thing in common. They were all safely and consistently vanilla. Whether or not that explained why the relationships never lasted was another story.

Sadie folded her long legs, skinny jeans creaking at the knee. "Does he know he's not the only one?" It was an oblique way of asking if Hazel had come clean with her dirty little secret. That Sadie even bothered couching it in vagueness was a sign of how well she understood the trickiness of the subject.

"Not sure that's first date conversation..."

"You have to tell him."

"Why?"

Sadie quirked an eloquent eyebrow.

*Oh.* "Yes. Fine. Yeah, it's part of the reason I'm attracted to him," Hazel groaned. Then quickly added, "But I don't know that it's something I want to do again." *With him. With anyone. Ever.*

Most days, she was happier not thinking about it at all. Those cravings would go away eventually.

"If… Okay, hypothetically speaking? If you were to jump back into that particular pool, you could do a lot worse than Dylan." Sadie pursed her lips around the straw. Then she tapped a finger against the cup, meditatively. "I know you don't want details, so I'm only going to say this once. He's a good Dom. You'd be in safe hands. And his playroom—"

Hazel held up a hand, grimacing. "Okay. I appreciate what you're trying to do, but no. I can't hear that from you."

"I'm only trying to help…"

"I know and I'm grateful." Somehow, her voice didn't shake. "But I can't be thinking of you and him together. Not yet. Maybe not ever, I don't know." Too much had happened since high school. Hazel wasn't that gullible, naïve girl anymore. She knew her hard limits.

She didn't have many friends besides Sadie. Something like this—a kernel of doubt, the seed of envy blooming in the pit of her stomach whenever she compared herself to Sadie—could end their friendship.

Sadie opened her mouth, closed it and nodded at the floor.

"We need ground rules," Hazel went on.

"Kinky."

She ignored Sadie's quip. "No talk about Dylan's playroom. I don't want to know what's in there, what he does or how he does it." *Not even if it helps me mentally prepare.*

Sadie grinned, resting the tip of the green straw on her tongue. "But he does it *really* well."

"Rule number two, if I try any of…that with him, I'll do it in my own time. And I tell him when I'm ready." *If I'm ready.*

"There's a good chance we'll be old and gray by then, but sure." Sadie shook her head. "Your body, your choice… Right, chicken?"

Hazel flipped her off. "Rule number three, if any of this makes you uncomfortable, tell me and I won't bring it up again."

"Why would your completely rational…irrational hang-ups make *me* uncomfortable?"

"You know what I mean." Sadie could be flippant and mulish in her own relationships, but they had never experimented with seeing the same guy – albeit at different times. Hazel usually appreciated her mean streak, but this time it made her feel a little wary. "I don't want to lose you because of some guy."

Sadie rubbed a finger under her glossy lower lip, as though considering this. "You're worrying for nothing. I'm totally cool with it."

"Okay. Good." Hazel tilted her head against the backrest of the couch. She yearned to believe it could be that simple.

"Frank and I are doing great, by the way," Sadie added with the twist of a smile. "Thanks for asking."

Hazel arched her eyebrows. "Like you need me to ask… Did you finally take him for a drive?"

Sadie's grin was ear-splitting, an answer unto itself. Her methods of seduction were limited to acting as crazy as possible or as flirtatious as possible – driving up the winding ribbon of highway that wreathed the Santa Monica Mountains fulfilled both quotas. Lately, she took Hazel's car for those outings, having wrapped her own around a tree last spring.

Nine lives, she'd say whenever Hazel urged her to ease up on the gas. Sometimes she listened. Mostly, she just gunned the engine and rolled the windows down, choosing to think of speed limits as suggestions.

Hazel sighed into her latte. "Here's hoping you filled up the tank."

# Chapter Five

Tuesday mornings at Marco's were noisy, chaotic affairs, even more so than the usual. Tuesdays was the day he got to see his daughter, which meant he took off in the morning to drive her to school and didn't come back until well after eight o'clock. Hazel had the run of the kitchen. She was never happier than when he finally breezed into the diner all wide grin and puffed up chest, *il straoridinario papà*.

"You look like you've seen Jesus," he teased, leaning on the counter that separated diner from kitchen.

"Don't let it go to your head." Hazel brushed perspiration from her brow with her sleeve. "Are you going to stay there and gawp for the rest of the day?"

"It's tempting," Marco admitted with a crooked grin.

Sadie nudged him out of the way with her hip. If she noticed his blush, she hid it well.

"Two hash browns, one large, one peppered, and one pecan waffle. And I'm still waiting for that sausage and cheese wrap," she added in a singsong, perfectly matching the cheap muzak Marco insisted on pumping through the speakers duct-taped to the rafters.

Hazel nodded, trying to find herself in the sizzling patties on the grill.

"Step aside," Marco ordered, "and behold the master at work." He donned his apron with a flourish and claimed the spatula from Hazel's hands as though taking up a scepter.

Seeing his kid didn't just put him in a good mood. It turned him into a nicer guy.

Come evening, the pendulum would swing all the way in the other direction at the thought of driving his daughter back to her mother's. Hazel was used to the seesaw. It was why Sadie usually worked Tuesday evenings. For now, she was just glad for the break.

Hazel pushed out of the swiveling kitchen doors and slipped through the back door of the diner, gulping down breaths. The alley stank of dumpster refuse and cat piss—still preferable to the cloying, overpowering sweetness of pancakes and waffles.

It was a beautiful day outside, much nicer than the one before. Summer had finally come to the west coast. Hazel leaned against the brick wall of the diner and turned her gaze toward the sky. Puffy white clouds drifted by on a blue backdrop, like something out of a child's coloring book.

She didn't hear the sound of footsteps until they aborted and turned back toward the mouth of the alley.

"Hazel? Is that you?" Dylan squinted, his expression twisted as if he'd smelled bad fish. It was entirely possible.

"In all my overworked glory," Hazel replied. She was technically supposed to be working, but Marco wouldn't mind her taking a break. She'd covered for him all morning. "What are you doing here?" she asked, sidestepping oily, rainbow puddles to meet Dylan on the sidewalk. Standing near him was a constant reminder that she'd let herself go—the hairnet she was currently sporting and the pungent whiff of melted cheese didn't help.

He swayed toward her, then away again, as though he couldn't decide between kissing her and giving her space.

"Breakfast. I called to ask if it was okay, but..."

"My phone's somewhere in my locker," Hazel explained. She had given him her cell number when it might have been smarter to give him the diner's. "Everything okay?"

"I think that's my line." Dylan smiled warmly.

"Almost didn't recognize you without the suit," Hazel quipped, ogling him unabashedly. Maybe it counted as objectification—maybe not—but Dylan didn't need a tailored suit to look a million bucks.

He glanced down at himself, as if only then noticing that he'd dug out a pair of jeans from his closet instead of donning his usual Hugo Boss armor. "Yeah, I took the day off."

"Guess you were hoping last night would turn out a little differently, huh?"

He waved a hand. "Let's not live in the past."

"I'm free tonight," Hazel ventured cheekily. Sadie owed her one, anyway.

Dylan grimaced at the traffic whizzing past in a ceaseless succession of foreign cars. Marco's hole in the wall was strategically perched on the main back road that tied LA to Newport, one of many wannabe pit stops on the scrap of urban decrepitude that had sprung up at the far edge of the city. If not for Sadie, Dylan might never have set foot inside. Hazel might never have contemplated throwing boiling hot coffee into his face.

She wouldn't be thinking of kissing him now.

"Actually," he started, "that's something I wanted to talk to you about…"

Dread bloomed in the pit of Hazel's stomach. "Tonight's no good for you?"

"My roommate wants to meet you."

"Come again?" She'd heard him the first time, but when deciphered, the request made no sense. Dylan's *arrangement* was his problem. She didn't have a stake in that and it had nothing to do with her.

He shifted his weight, as uncomfortable as Hazel felt. "I… I told him about us. About you. After I got back, we talked. *A lot.*"

*Wait, there's an* us?

"And at some point in that talk he decided he wanted to meet up?" Patience was not one of Hazel's strongest suits. Dread listed dangerously into panic the more she stood there, hanging on Dylan's every word.

"It's your call."

"I'd be worried if it wasn't."

Dylan smiled crookedly. "If you're up for it, he suggested dinner. Tonight."

"I'm not cooking for three," Hazel quipped. "Not enough plates." Plus, her apartment felt cramped enough with two people in it. With three, they'd suffocate.

"I know a place."

She was aware that she was equivocating. Dylan would probably take no for an answer. He might even agree to another date—just for the two of them—to make it up to her. The more time they spent together the more he seemed like a genuinely decent person.

*Trusting your instincts again, are you?* quipped a self-sabotaging voice at the back of her mind. *You know they're not worth shit.*

"Okay." She let out a long breath. "Pick me up from the apartment at eight."

Dylan had no business heaving a sigh of relief when it was Hazel who was being asked to play nice with the in-laws—or the creepy, homo-romantic roommate equivalent. And yet it felt good to know she'd lifted a weight off his shoulders. So much so that she found herself smiling when he did, pleased to have been of service.

"Still want to come in for breakfast or...?" Hazel trailed off, hitching up her shoulders.

"I just wanted to see you," Dylan admitted sheepishly. "Breakfast was an excuse."

Wings fluttered in the cage of Hazel's ribs. She ignored the ticklish sensation. Just hours ago, she'd told Sadie she didn't know what she wanted out of this *thing* with Dylan—if anything at all. It had started out as a harmless bit of fun. A dare.

She wasn't daring herself with the squirming in her chest or the heat in her cheeks. Those were all warning signs, a five-alarm carillon she couldn't afford to ignore.

The diner door clanged open, bell chimes swinging. The sound brought her crashing down to earth. "Okay, well... I should get back to work."

"I won't keep you."

"See you tonight," Hazel said, trying to inject enthusiasm into her voice. If nothing else, it would be a great opportunity to spend more time with Dylan—while getting grilled by his weird, not so platonic roommate. "Hey, I didn't ask," she called, one hand already on the diner door. "Did your car make it through the night okay?"

Dylan spun around, hands tucked into his pockets. He might have been a cutout from a Levi's commercial. Hazel's mouth went dry. "Yeah," he replied. "Why?"

*I'm pretty sure I dreamed of us in the back seat?* Hazel shrugged. "And you?"

He smiled ruefully and waved a hand from side to side as if to say *so-so*. "See you tonight." With that, he turned and walked off the same way he'd come.

Hazel stepped into the cacophony of the diner, trying not to feel like she'd just agreed to leap out of a plane without a parachute.

\* \* \* \*

That forgotten bastion of quintessentially Midwestern values that was Dunby, Missouri had only ever had one diner and one bar for as long as Hazel remembered. Kids went to the former with their parents until they were old enough to sneak into the latter with their friends.

A town of barely two hundred souls had little concept of price range or competition. If the old ranchers turned wealthy paragons of the community wanted to feast, they either crossed the Mississippi and drove to Dyersburg or Union City, or stayed in their sprawling mansions and reveled in home-cooked meals prepared by their live-in staff. The poor had a similar choice, albeit between soup kitchens in the greater townships or canned soup at home.

The same rules didn't apply to places like LA. Hazel was never more aware of this than when she stood outside a restaurant clearly above her pay grade, with a man who was clearly out of her league. *Maybe this wasn't such a good idea.* She felt ill at ease in her too-tight black dress, the girdle underneath cutting her airflow even as her heart pumped faster, trying to keep pace with her racing thoughts.

Dylan pressed a hand to the small of her back. "Shall we?"

The doors slid open as if he'd whispered 'Open Sesame'. The distinct absence of muzak struck Hazel first then the white-clad maître d', who smiled at Dylan like an old friend. She watched them shake hands, but whatever words they exchanged flew right over her head. She was too preoccupied with taking in the chandeliers casting warm yellow beams onto wood paneled walls and white tablecloths alike.

In a pinch, she might have called it industrial espionage, though it would take a serious windfall for Marco's to become even a pale shadow of this place.

And if it did, Marco's first managerial decision would probably be to replace the likes of her with proper wait staff.

The tables were arranged in a horseshoe, three rows converging around a dance floor where couples of all ages were waltzing discreetly to the warble of a live band. The parallels to Buddy's wedding were so strong that Hazel nearly started combing the crowd for signs of the bride and groom.

The maître d' led them through the restaurant like wayward pups.

Hazel kept her arm linked through Dylan's and an eye out for a single man at a table set for three. Her pulse throbbed frantically between her ears. She wasn't entirely sure she wouldn't pass out before the fateful meeting. *That would be very, very dumb. You're a grown woman. This guy doesn't mean anything to you.*

The problem—she was beginning to see—was that she wasn't as indifferent to Dylan as she might have liked. Passing muster with his friends mattered.

"Mr. Parrish?" The maître d' bent discreetly over a black-clad shoulder. "Your party is here."

Hazel had anticipated an older man—some sort of white-haired sugar daddy who drove a BMW and dictated whom Dylan could see in his private time. It was a bit of a stretch sure, since nothing about Dylan suggested he *needed* a benefactor, but Hazel couldn't wrap her mind around it otherwise.

She gawped as Parrish startled to his feet. He couldn't have been older than Dylan. He stood maybe an inch shorter—though that might have been a consequence of his slouching—and wore his blond hair in riotous, short-sheared curls. Like Dylan, he knew how to fill a suit—and the resemblance didn't end there. He had the same knowing eyes, the same penetrating stare. His dimples were like parentheses denting his improbably sharp cheeks when he grinned.

But where Dylan was gorgeous and magnetic like a dazzling sun, Parrish put Hazel in mind of Old Testament fables and a jealous God. She found herself staring at his perfect mouth with all its straight, white teeth. She imagined she could see old blood and sinew caught in the gaps around his canines.

"Dylan! Ah, and this must be Hazel." He held out a broad, white palm. "I've heard a lot about you."

"Well, that's good... Me, I've heard *nothing* about you, Mr. Parrish," Hazel shot back, pumping his fingers in a sure grip. *You don't scare me.*

The arch reply only broadened his smile. "Ward, please. We'll have to see about remedying that oversight, won't we?" He released her hand without preamble.

Dylan pulled up a chair for her on Ward's right. She sat down carefully, hoping against hope that the fraying seams of the dress would last out the night.

"So what's good here?" Hazel quipped. "I'm guessing it's not your first time."

"We don't have many of those left," Ward countered. He alone didn't pick up his menu. "I recommend the fennel soup, perhaps followed by the roasted sole. And a waltz, of course. Do you dance, Hazel?"

"Not if it involves choreography."

"Ah, but with a firm hand to lead you, there should be no need."

Hazel slanted a glance across the table at Dylan. How much did Ward know about her, exactly? "I'm not really interested in being *led* by anyone, but thanks. I think I'll have the salmon." She folded the menu shut. "And I'll skip the wine."

Dylan sucked the corners of his lips in. "So will I."

"You're joking," Ward scoffed. He had a faint accent, not British but not American, either. "You're *not* joking?" He frowned. "Well, this is a sad day. I'm glad I didn't order champagne."

He flagged down the nearest waiter. "Change of plans. Forget the wine. Bring me a Scotch instead."

"Yes, sir."

Ward had such ease with barking orders that Hazel was willing to bet money he was an only child—a *pampered* only child, at that. This was what spoiled little tyrants grew up to become. It didn't explain why Dylan smiled so fondly in his direction whenever Ward was focused on something else.

*Stockholm Syndrome is a thing.*

It struck her suddenly that if she'd seen them together from the first, she wouldn't have given Dylan the time of day for all the free dinners in the world.

"It seems I owe you an apology," Ward announced out of the blue, training his arresting gaze on Hazel. A pair of lasers would've unsettled her less. "Dylan explained what happened last night. Had I known, I would've stayed another night in San Diego."

"I didn't want to put you out of your home..."

He waved a hand, dismissing the apology. "You wouldn't have. There are two levels to the loft, and the walls have been decently soundproofed." Ward smiled when the waiter deposited his Scotch on the table. He tapped a finger to the edge of the tumbler, looking like a man who enjoyed drinking but knew that he needed to pace himself.

*This one's the control freak.* Which meant Dylan was what? The sidekick? The enabler?

The accomplice?

Hazel buried her apprehension deep. She had watched enough TV to know that pairs of serial killers were rare. More than that, she wanted to believe Dylan was a good egg. Why else would he have encouraged her to send Sadie a text when they got to the restaurant?

That indefatigable voice at the back of her mind whispered that he was obviously trying to make Sadie jealous. That it was *her* he wanted all along. But he wasn't introducing Sadie to his friends. He wasn't mouthing 'sorry' at her as Ward launched into a convoluted tale about the loft's history as a shoe polish manufacturer's and a speakeasy before it came into their possession.

Hazel pretended to listen, but she couldn't shake the suspicion that Ward was pulling double duty, at once playing master of ceremonies and observer.

She was relieved when the moment came to order.

"So, Mr. Parrish," she said in the ensuing lull, "what is it you do?"

"Ward," he corrected with a flinty sneer. "Have you heard of Apex Engineering?"

The name rang faintly in her memory. "Weren't they the guys who took all that government money only for the CEO to go down on tax evasion charges?" She followed the news, but only because Marco liked to have the radio on in the kitchen. He despised the music he inflicted on his patrons.

Ward smiled thinly. "The CEO was my father."

"Oh." *Insert foot in mouth.*

"I inherited the mess when he went to prison."

"So you're a CEO."

"At the ripe age of thirty-three," Ward confirmed, raising his whiskey glass. "Feel free to let your astonishment show. I hear some variation of 'you're much too young for the job' every other day of the week. This one," he added, jerking his head toward Dylan, "keeps telling me to sell and wash my hands of the whole putrid business."

Dylan arched his eyebrows and sighed. "You ask my opinion."

"I keep hoping it'll change."

"You always were an optimist."

The look they shared was at odds with their body language. Hazel couldn't help but think of feral beasts that hunt together, then lick each other's fur clean of the blood spatter. *I guess that makes me prey...* It wasn't the most flattering mental image.

"Can't be easy," she mused, "feeling like everyone's ganging up against you." Whether or not it was the case was another story, but paranoia was popular among the powerful even when their parents weren't indicted felons.

"Not *everyone*," Ward scoffed.

He didn't need to smile at Dylan for Hazel to understand that she was the third wheel to their homoerotic love-fest. She wanted to feel affronted, but it wasn't as if Dylan hadn't told her that his relationship with Ward was complex. He'd done his best to prepare her. As late as the drive to the restaurant, he'd told her repeatedly that he could call Ward and cancel. His gaze was wary even now, as if he expected his eccentric friend to lash out. Like he thought Hazel might react badly to the company.

"Must be hard knowing who to trust," she added, fingering the stem of her water glass.

"It is," Ward agreed. "That's why I keep Dylan around."

*Now we're getting somewhere.*

"Interesting choice of words."

Ward smirked, sharklike, behind his tumbler. "Spoken like a true English major."

Icy fingers cast down Hazel's spine. She fought not to flinch. "You looked me up."

"Just keeping an eye out for my friend's wellbeing. That's all."

"Ward—"

A raised finger curbed Dylan's objection. Ward wasn't finished. "It's nothing personal. Dylan so rarely gets attached that when it happens, I'm extremely wary of anyone who might be trying to use him. Don't worry, I didn't hire private detectives to follow you around. I Googled."

Hazel would've preferred the private dicks. There was only so much they could dig up from her daily routine. For a twenty-six-year-old in a city with a decent nightlife, she led an exceptionally boring existence. Six years ago would have been a whole other matter. And those pictures *were* still cached somewhere. They certainly popped up a lot.

*If not the pics, then the video. Christ…*

She leaned forward, twisting to face Ward head on. "And what's your conclusion? *Am* I using your friend? I mean he washed my dishes last night, so that's like…a step below stealing his credit card and going crazy at Nordstrom, right?" Her voice shook. She couldn't help it.

Ward still wore that infuriating smile — the same one that made her want to punch his teeth in. Not, on reflection, a good way to endear Dylan to her.

"Just as long as you don't actually let him cook. He once tried to boil water in the dorm kitchen and nearly burned the building down around us."

"In my defense," said Dylan, "I was high."

"You put a plastic bottle in the microwave."

"It was a very old microwave!"

"Yet it survived twenty-five years of idiot boys… Until you." Ward shook his head, but his expression was fond when he turned to Hazel. "He has other uses around the house. For instance, he's wonderful with pets or small children. And he can reach high shelves. If you have any curtains that need putting up, he's your man."

"Are you trying to sell him?" Hazel quirked her eyebrows, feigning ignorance. *I know what you're up to* played like a mantra between her ears. It hadn't escaped her that Ward hadn't answered the question.

*He knows. He knows and he's saving it to lord over you if you get too serious about Dylan.* It was a sobering thought.

"More like rent me out," Dylan muttered under his breath, oblivious. "I'm not a piece of meat, you know. I have *feelings.*"

Ward rolled his eyes. "So says the man who spends his days tallying other people's money."

"Ah, what better way to skim from the top? But you'd know that, wouldn't you?"

Ward pressed a hand to his chest. "And my heart goes crack."

"What heart?" Dylan pouted.

The frantic thump of Hazel's pulse began to beat at a steadier cadence. Dylan and Ward seemed content ribbing each other. After initial hostilities had been exchanged, Ward left off trying to threaten her into playing nice.

The first course was brought out—fennel soup, as per Ward's recommendation—while he regaled them with tales of his baboon board members.

He was one of those men who enjoy the sound of their own voice. He did it so faithfully that he barely seemed to taste the soup. Hazel thought about suggesting they swap plates because the velvety cream was sort of addictive, but she refrained.

Her dress was tight enough already.

The main course dashed her hopes of slaking her hunger on anything more consistent. Two medallions of salmon and a thin strip of black rice did not a supper make.

"Should have had the sole," Ward said when the waiter came to retrieve their plates.

"Free will is a beautiful thing," Dylan countered. "And on that note." He flashed Hazel a smile. "If I promise to let you lead, would you do me the honor of this dance?"

"I don't want to say that you sound like a time traveler from the eighteen hundreds, but..." Ward held up his hands when Hazel glowered.

Perhaps it would've annoyed him to be thwarted yet again. Perhaps he wouldn't have cared. Either way, Hazel slid her chair back and stood. "Let's go, Mr. Darcy."

Dylan followed her onto the dance floor as the in-house pianist started on the first notes of Nat King Cole's *Unforgettable*.

*Yep, definitely feels like Buddy's wedding.*

She banished the pang of guilt she felt at the thought of Rhonda and the baby shower. After her mother's call, Hazel had wound up declining the invite on Facebook, in the most impersonal way she could possibly have replied.

Thanksgiving would be interesting this year.

"I'm sorry he's so difficult," Dylan whispered in her ear as he pulled her close. "If you want to leave..."

Hazel wrapped an arm around his shoulders and let Dylan fold his hand around her wrist. "Already? But I'm having such fun." It wasn't a complete lie. Ward had 'life of the party' practically stamped on his forehead. He wasn't *likable*, but he was entertaining. Hazel had no desire to capitulate just because he'd annoyed her a bit. "You've known him for a long time, haven't you?"

Dylan hummed a note of acquiescence, the sound bubbling out from deep within his chest.

"We met in freshman year. That's... God, is that really twelve years ago?" He shook his head, brushing her temple with his lips. "He's a good guy. A little standoffish, but a good guy."

*If you say so.* It wasn't Dylan's past that Ward had gone digging into.

"And will he be a good guy at the loft tonight, or… Is he going back to San Diego, by any chance?"

She felt Dylan's smile more than saw it. "I think he's headed back."

"Excellent."

"Yeah?" Dylan spun her under his arm. "You have designs on my virtue, do you?"

Hazel shook her head. "It'll all be very spontaneous. Not like I spent all day thinking about it—or you."

"Oh, really?" Dylan tipped forward, close enough to press a delicate, chaste kiss to the hinge of her jaw. "That makes two of us."

"How narcissistic."

His chuckle gusted against her cheek, rippling like a caress across her skin. She wanted nothing more than to kiss him as he pulled back, but Dylan didn't stop at a few inches. When he turned, Hazel glimpsed Ward over his shoulder.

"May I cut in?"

Dylan hesitated, wary puzzlement on his handsome face.

"Sure," said Hazel. There was no other polite answer she could give. Ward would be offended if she refused and, hands down, he'd win Dylan in the custody battle. He'd known him longer.

Appropriately, the house band transitioned into the eponymous *Habanera* as Ward offered his hand. She took it. "I don't tango."

"Neither do I," Ward replied. "But if I were to learn with someone, I could do worse."

"What's that supposed to mean?"

"That I'm a fan of your work."

Couples of all ages swayed and twirled around them, some more skillfully than others. Hazel remained mostly stationary. *At least it's a short piece.* Even on an empty stomach, she still would've felt a little sick standing there, like a rabbit who'd misguidedly ventured into the foxhole.

"You don't like me very much," Ward noted when she didn't respond.

"I don't know you." The not so civilized variant? *I think you're a manipulative Ritchie Rich. Whatever hold you've got over Dylan, it won't work with me.* Hazel swallowed it back, because it wasn't true, not a bit. She'd run from men with far fewer resources at their disposal than Ward Parrish and she was still looking over her shoulder. "I don't even know where you're from."

"Pretoria."

"South Africa?" Hazel smiled thinly. "Huh. Of course, *you* don't need to ask the same question. Google already told you."

Ward hummed a note of acquiescence, his palm warm on the small of her back. "Google told me many things. For instance, turns out there's some interesting material of you on certain websites..."

Hazel's feet became rooted to the floor. Her blood congealed in her veins. "What do you want?"

Ward's gaze was more pitying than cruel, as though he was disappointed that she had confirmed his suspicions. Perhaps he would've preferred staunch denials. Perhaps he expected Hazel to make a scene. But what would be the point?

His forbearing sigh did nothing to shift the chill that had slithered into Hazel's bones.

"A dance, Ms. Whitley. Nothing more."

Hazel made herself move. *Dance, monkey, dance.* Inside, she was screaming.

# Chapter Six

The Tesla slid to a seamless stop. The engine's subsonic hum gave way to silence. Cars still whistled past them, rattling the sedan with their speed.

Hazel startled when Dylan took her hand.

"You're very quiet tonight," he opined. It was a tentative overture and so unlike the man who'd brazenly written his phone number out on a cheap paper napkin—or picked Sadie up in a fetish club. "Is everything—?"

"Just tired, I guess." The lie had legs. She'd worked from eight that morning to six in the evening. She hadn't had much of a weekend. She'd spent the evening making nice with Dylan's boyfriend-cum-roommate.

"Want me to drive you home?"

Dylan's offer seemed genuine, much like the rest of him, but Hazel shook her head.

She followed Dylan out of the car, shivering a little until he wrapped an arm around her waist and pulled her against his flank. They had to part again to negotiate the stairs, but just for a moment, Hazel could inhale his cologne and revel in his body heat. Her vision blurred.

This could never work.

She'd blinked away the tears by the time Dylan led them into the loft. It was, as Ward had boasted, a large, sprawling apartment. The scant, sleek furniture made it seem even grander. Everything, from the bare brick walls to the curtain-less windows, was utilitarian, cold. A metal staircase right of the front door led up to a second story. Ward's domain, Hazel guessed.

Her heels made soft clicking noises on the bare hardwood floors. She'd spotted the austere, grunge-chic lines when she'd come to pick Sadie up all those weeks before. Being inside was a different story, though. There was a game console under the TV, for one thing. And a pizza carton rested conspicuously on the kitchen island.

"Do you want something to drink?" Dylan asked, sliding the front door shut and securing the latch. "I have coffee—"

"I want to see your playroom."

He froze, a deer in the headlights look snagging on his features. "Okay..." He flicked a hand toward a corridor left of the door. As best Hazel could tell, the loft wrapped around the main stairwell, more L-shaped than strictly square. Bookshelves lined the walls, overflowing with brick-size paperbacks. Hazel kept an eye out for de Sade, but all she could make out were mystery writers.

Someone—either Dylan or Ward—had an obvious fondness for Agatha Christie.

The bedroom Dylan led her into was in no way extraordinary. Between the four white-painted walls and the gray rug, Hazel wondered if she'd been duped. The walnut-framed bed didn't even have a headboard. She noticed *Sleeping Murder* on the nightstand, though, which elucidated the enigma of the bookshelves outside.

Yet Dylan didn't stop in the bedroom. He marched to one of four doors leading out of the room and turned the handle. Hazel glimpsed bare brick and a St. Andrew's cross.

*Jackpot.*

Insides churning uncomfortably, she trailed Dylan to the doorframe. That niggling voice at the back of her mind dared her to step over the threshold. It goaded. Hazel slid a foot forward, then the other, and let out a noisy breath.

"In case it's not obvious," Dylan said, "you should know I had no intention of concluding our evening in here."

"Why not?" Hazel shot over her shoulder. Some men mounted stag heads or foot-long trout on their walls. Dylan had hung up whips and paddles and floggers of every size. Judging by the chains that crisscrossed the ceiling, he wasn't averse to a little suspension play to go with the hardcore impact fun.

"It would be a little presumptuous, for one thing... And we haven't talked about this."

"What's there to talk about?"

Dylan shifted his weight, the impeccable lines of his worsted wool suit rustling as he stuck his hands into his trouser pockets. "Are you interested in kink?"

"Yes." The answer was a sigh. Yes, she was interested. Yes, she was *terrified*. Hazel picked up a pair of padded leather handcuffs. "Looks like I'm not the only one."

The tension in the room ratcheted up a notch as Dylan bridged the gap between them with a few short steps. He closed his hand around Hazel's, trapping the cuffs in the palm of her hand. The spicy, earthy tones of his cologne seeped into her lungs as though her skin was permeable. His scent snared her. She tipped forward.

Dylan stopped her with a hand at her waist. "Are you sure about this?"

"Positive." There might not be another chance, if Ward got his way.

His gaze darted probingly over her face. Hazel fought not to look away. She was sure he could feel her pulse racing in her wrist.

"What's your safe word?"

His voice rippled down her spine like a pin digging into a particularly sensitive nerve.

"Um… Nothing comes to mind."

It wasn't a lie. Her hindbrain had taken over the minute she'd stepped over the threshold. Everything here was a turn-on and everything was triggering. If Dylan released her hand, she was sure she'd fall to her knees.

Dylan frowned. "Do you know the stoplight system? Red for stop, green for go, yellow if you're not sure?"

"I do now." And because talking was becoming difficult, Hazel leaned in and pressed her lips to his. She'd been yearning to kiss him since they'd parted ways last night. She might have dreamed of it if not for liquor swaddling her thoughts in black.

Except that wasn't true. *Everyone dreams, some people just don't remember.* And for the most part, Hazel was relieved when she'd woken up with mind blank and no creeping revulsion in the pit of her stomach.

When she was awake, she could beat back the unfortunate sensation of wanting something she knew she couldn't have.

Dylan tightened his hand in her hair.

"That's enough from you," he rasped, voice dropping an octave.

The rebuke elicited a small shiver, but nothing near as bad as the full-body shiver that arced through her when Dylan broke away. He circled like a hawk. The hand he'd used to clasp her waist slid down to the small of her back, then up again, over the line of the concealed zipper to seize the plastic stub at her nape. He tugged it down slowly, metal teeth clicking open one by one, until the dress fell open.

Hazel flexed her hands at her sides. If she were slimmer, the fabric would just glide down her body. She could kick it aside, and stand there looking sexy in her black lingerie.

At least this time she'd had the foresight to make sure her bra and underwear matched. A pity she'd forgotten about the girdle.

It was a revolting, scratchy torture device the color of dishwater. Heat flooded her cheeks as Dylan eased the dress the rest of the way down her thighs. He gave a sharp tug when it caught on her hips and the fabric obediently slid loose. Hazel fanned her toes inside her pumps for balance. She thought about sucking in her stomach, but that wouldn't do any good.

"I'm sorry," tore out of her before she could bite back the sentiment.

Dylan's touch stilled at the edge of the girdle. "For?"

He was going to make her say it? "I'm wearing this goddamn thing." *I bet Sadie doesn't need one. I bet you peeled her out of her clothes like something out of a movie.* Bitterness choked her.

Maybe this was a mistake.

Dylan slid a knuckle under her chin and forced her to meet his gaze. "Did I say you could speak?"

Air left Hazel's breath in a rush. "No."

"No," he repeated. The order was implicit. *So don't.*

He trailed a fingertip down the bumps in her spine, only pausing to unclasp her bra. By the time he'd reached her ample hips again, his breath was already gusting hot against Hazel's nape. He hooked two fingers in the sides of the girdle and rolled it down. The elastic fibers snagged on her curves. Hazel's cheeks warmed, then numbed when she felt Dylan breathe out a laugh.

"Making me work for it, I see…" He kissed the slope of her shoulder.

Hazel shivered, mortification only two-thirds of the feelings roiling in the pit of her stomach. Only once it had passed her thighs did the girdle roll down her legs and slip the rest of the way off. The black bra followed soon after, robbing her of much needed padding.

The sudden urge to cover up came and went without Hazel doing anything to assuage it.

"I like the pantyhose," Dylan purred, raking his fingernails over her hips as if to amplify the whisper of silk and skin. "But I think I'd like you better without them."

Hazel disagreed, but somehow the comeback stuck in her throat. Already she was relearning the rules about not speaking unless asked a direct question. It should have frightened her that she could so easily fit back into that mold.

It didn't.

Dylan crouched to roll her stockings down, pausing only when he reached her ankles. Goosebumps bloomed over Hazel's skin as he helped her out of the black pumps. The floor was warm beneath her toes. Perhaps a hot water pipe passed underneath.

Anything was possible with these old buildings—including paper-thin walls.

Hazel bit her lower lip when she felt Dylan stroke his hands up the backs of her knees. Her legs nearly buckled.

"Ticklish?" Dylan asked and Hazel could hear the smile in his voice. "Good to know."

Did he not have eyes? Was he disappointed that she wasn't as slim and toned as Sadie? Did he regret bringing her here in the first place?

Thoughts obliterated as he stood with a sigh and pressed his clothed, perfect body against her back. Hazel bit back a moan, swaying listlessly. She could feel his cock through his slacks. His *hard* cock.

Dylan slid an arm around her waist and pressed his lips to her ear. "Do you like to be told what we're going to do or do you want it to be a surprise?"

"Tell me," Hazel got out tremulously, figuring she was permitted to speak as long as she was answering a direct question. She didn't know what she liked—not anymore—but now wasn't the time to have that conversation. There was a very real danger that Dylan might stop if she brought it up.

He brushed a lock of hair from Hazel's shoulder, baring her neck to his lips. "I'd like to tie your hands over your head and go down on you. How does that sound?"

*Pretty fucking amazing.* Hazel swallowed hard. "I'd like that."

She could feel him grinning into her shoulder blade.

"Good." He took the handcuffs from her hand and slid one leather manacle around her wrist. If he noticed her shiver as he fastened the buckle, he didn't let on.

Hazel inhaled sharply as he guided her arms up and over her head, clipping the length of chain between them to a hook in the ceiling.

"Give it a tug," Dylan whispered in her ear.

She did. The leather bit into the skin, but because the cuffs covered so much width, it felt more like an Indian burn than a sharp, piercing sting. Most importantly, the hook held fast. Hazel felt a panicky whimper build in her chest. She had just allowed a man she barely knew to tie her up in his scary, BDSM dungeon. She was all but naked, on display before him like a piece of meat.

And though Sadie knew she'd gone out to dinner with Dylan and his 'friend', she didn't know that Hazel had wound up at Dylan's. She wouldn't know to come here.

She wouldn't get here in time.

*In time for what?*

Hazel's worst fears were a hazy, amorphous *what if*, her thoughts snarling into a tangled web as the pressure in her chest intensified.

The dread building at her core nearly spilled out.

Then Dylan stepped into her field of vision, peeling off his jacket. Nothing remotely scary about him. He was the same guy who'd done dishes at her apartment out of some bizarre notion of chivalry. He'd refused to sleep with her because she'd had a couple of drinks.

Those wicked black eyes were crinkled when he turned back to face Hazel, sleeves rucked up to the elbow and his throat bobbing with ill-disguised excitement.

"I can hear you thinking from all the way over here… You nervous?"

Hazel shook her head, hair spilling over her shoulder in curling strands. She was so hyper-aware that even the idle touch of his hand brushing the ringlets away from her face sent a zing of pleasure straight to her cunt.

"Good. You shouldn't be." Dylan dragged his fingertips down the swell of her breast, cautiously avoiding her nipple. He smirked when Hazel squirmed, swaying languidly between floor and ceiling hook, and laughed when she moaned as he pinched her nipple between thumb and forefinger. "Something to say? By all means, don't edit yourself."

He scraped the blunt side of his nail into the sensitive nub of flesh, waiting for her whimper before letting go.

"You and I are going to have so much fun together."

Was that a backhanded compliment? Before Hazel could make up her mind, he was repeating the process with her other breast, alternating achingly sweet caresses with sharp, painful castigation. Hazel rocked back on her heels, torn between wanting to arch her back and offer herself up for more, and inching back as far as her bonds allowed to escape the torment.

Dylan made her mind up by wrapping an arm around her waist, fingers splayed against the swell of her ass, and dipping his mouth to her chest. If Hazel thought him kissing her lips was breathtaking, she'd been too quick to judge. Warmth pooled low in her belly, gushing out as she curled her toes into the floor.

"Oh, fuck, yes..." A ragged breath tore out of her lungs—close to, but not quite, a moan.

She never thought she could come from someone playing with her nipples before—the very idea seemed like *Cosmo* levels of pseudo-science—but with Dylan rolling his tongue against her flesh, she began to revise that firm denial. Every swipe of his teeth, every wet, mind-blowing suck had her inner muscles clenching around thin air, cunt begging to be filled. Her clit throbbed in time with the pendulum flick of Dylan's tongue. And just as her pleas rose to a crescendo, he pulled away.

Hazel groaned, breaths knifing in and out of her chest. "Bastard."

"Careful," he warned. "I have gags in here, too, you know."

Adrenaline pumping through her veins, Hazel found the oft-traveled road to alarm easy to scale. She sucked her lips between her teeth, clamping her jaw shut.

Dylan took her chin. "That's better." The kiss he planted on her cheek was gentle and wet. "Wouldn't want to have to punish you, would we?"

Hazel didn't know if it was safe to shake her head, so she didn't. *I'm at his mercy. He calls the shots. I obey.* It would've been simple to do, if that little voice at the back of her mind didn't keep up a steady stream of taunts whenever she started to get too comfortable in her bonds. *Look at you, independent woman... A little overweight, a little desperate. You think you're the kind of chick he usually goes for? You're an exotic dish. He'll want someone like Sadie when he's done with you. A palate cleanser.*

"Don't cross your legs," Dylan said, a note of caution in his voice.

Hazel hadn't even realized she was doing it. She had to force her knees apart as Dylan knelt in front of her. Could he see that fleshy bit over her hip bones? *Duh.* What about the dimples in her thighs, the ones that women's magazines kept telling her to exercise out every summer?

*Obviously.*

She wheezed when he kissed her knee, wrapping her hands around the metal chain that held her suspended. The links clicked like wind chimes. Dylan must've heard, because she felt him grin into the plump bit of flesh along her inner thigh.

"Anticipation is a terrible thing," he teased. "Absolutely terrible."

He went on to prove it as he painted a trail of soft, chaste kisses all the way to the apex of her thighs, then down again over her other leg. Despite her misgivings, Hazel felt arousal gush out of her, more turned on than she'd been in years. This was what she liked, how she liked it—the loss of control, breathtakingly scary and scarily easy to give into.

Dylan stroked a fingertip along the seam of her black panties, avoiding the crotch until Hazel trembled before him.

"Look at you, sopping wet and practically begging to be touched... Is this what you want?" He dug a knuckle between her folds, wet cotton dulling the sensation even as he zeroed in on her clit.

Hazel bucked into that single point of pressure, a gasp catching pitifully in her throat.

"You'd settle for something to grind against, you greedy little slut. Wouldn't you?" He removed his hand and Hazel lurched forward, chains clinking overhead.

When she didn't answer fast enough, Dylan lightly smacked her inner thigh.

"Yes," Hazel gasped. "Yes, please. Anything." It scared her that he'd struck her. It scared her even more that she'd enjoyed it.

It wasn't so long ago that she would've begged for a spanking.

She wasn't far from it now, but Dylan's orders on whether or not she was allowed to speak were contradictory, distracting. She couldn't risk it.

"Is that right? *Anything*? And here I thought you wanted me to get you off with my tongue..." He ducked his head against her cotton-covered pussy before she could reply and did just that.

Hazel whined, a decidedly unattractive sound, body going rigid under his ministrations. "Oh, God... Don't stop." *So much for following orders.*

Dylan didn't seem to be listening, because after just a few deliciously precise swipes of the tongue, he pulled back again. His lips were red, chin slick with her juices. "I said I'd go down on you," he remarked, albeit a little choked. "I didn't say I'd get you off."

Dismay sank like a block of cement in Hazel's gut. "No, please..." The churning pleasure building at her core ebbed back. Hazel panted. "Please. Come on. You have to."

She didn't realize her mistake until Dylan was standing, his fingers tight around her chin. "What did you say to me?" he growled. He looked dangerous.

He looked *furious*.

Hazel's voice fled, taking with it the air in her lungs and the last scraps of courage she had left. She wanted to sink into the heated floor.

"I think you need a reminder as to who's in charge here..." He pulled away so abruptly that Hazel swayed forward before she could steady herself. She tracked him with her gaze, dreading that he'd make good on his threat to gag her after all.

It was a little pathetic that she felt relieved when he took up a leather crop, bending it between his hands before letting it whip back into shape with a bone-chilling hiss.

"What color are you on?" Dylan asked, from well across the room.

Hazel frowned.

"Green, yellow, red?"

*Oh. That.* She had to think about it. "Yellow?"

Dylan's expression softened as he approached. "It doesn't hurt very much. Do you want to try it and see?"

The change was so swift, anger fleeing his features as though it had never been there at all. It nearly gave Hazel whiplash. She shook her head. "I've used one before." Less 'used', more 'had used *on* me', but the answer was the same. "Don't... Don't hold back on my account."

Dylan seemed a little unsure, but he didn't challenge her. Maybe that was against his rules, too.

Hazel didn't get the chance to put much more thought into it before Dylan pulled back the crop and flicked its flat, fly-swatter-like tip against her hip. A sharp sting exploded in her buttocks, heat skittering up her spine.

"Red?" Dylan asked, steadying her with fingers splayed wide against her belly.

Hazel swallowed hard. "Green." *Very* green. She tilted into the offending instrument, eager to prolong the burn before it numbed away.

Dylan got the message and struck her again.

By the third stroke, Hazel's flesh prickled with hurt. By the fifth, she could barely hear the crackle of the crop as it went singing through the air. Dylan cupped her mound, clearly less as a way to steady her and more in an attempt to cop a feel.

Hazel bent at the waist on a swat that lashed her breasts. "Ah—I'm gonna come if you don't stop." Her voice barely sounded like her own anymore—or maybe that was just the drumming in her ears, making everything else seem hazy and muffled.

"You *want* me to stop?" Dylan asked. He sounded more awed than amused, although the dividing line was so permeable that perhaps Hazel had it all wrong.

She didn't care. Her pride had fled with the first smack of the riding crop. The rest was sensation and delight, bliss simmering in the pit of her stomach like champagne bubbles as hurt bloomed fresh under her skin.

She shook her head.

"That's what I thought." Dylan switched the crop from hand to hand and stepped back a foot.

The first swat across her midriff had Hazel doubling over—or at least as far as she could, considering that she was dangling from a hook in the ceiling. Her foot came up off the ground in a futile, thoughtless defense. It had been a while since she'd learned how to smother such instincts, but Dylan didn't seem to mind. He swatted her shin, then the back of her thigh when she only curled up tighter in a foolish attempt to protect herself.

Her ribcage rose and fell like a bellows.

"Put your foot down," Dylan ordered. "Now, Hazel." The rough cadences of his voice brooked no opposition, admitted no delay.

Hazel slammed her foot into the floor, curling her toes into the hardwood boards like that might help anchor them. It didn't. This was all about willpower and self-control, and Hazel had neither. She couldn't even follow a simple request. She couldn't do anything right. She was going to fuck this up and Dylan would be so disappointed. He wouldn't want to see her again.

Ward Parrish would get to feel vindicated about being right all along.

The pace of the slaps intensified, building to a crescendo along the underside of her breasts, then ceasing abruptly. Dylan tossed the crop to the floor and knelt. He would've ripped her panties off if they were of higher quality, but the cheap, sopping cotton held out in the face of his brutal tug. He didn't bother pulling them off completely, simply let them dangle around one ankle as he pressed his mouth to Hazel's cunt.

As per orders, she couldn't lift a foot off the ground. A moment later, it didn't matter.

Dylan was merciless, spearing his tongue to part her folds and lapping at her with sloppy, inexpert flicks, as if he couldn't set aside desire long enough to focus on what he was doing. Wet, vulgar noises ricocheted against the walls as he fastened his lips tightly around her clit. She tried to resist, but between the hot burn of the crop and his enthusiastic ministrations, it didn't take much to send Hazel over the edge.

She came like that, suspended from a hook in the ceiling. Her knees gave out at last. A sob tore from her throat as bittersweet ecstasy took her under.

It might have been a minute or an hour later that she felt Dylan rise, petting her flesh with gentle hands when she swayed against him. He undid the buckles on the leather cuffs easily, as if it was child's play. It occurred to Hazel that she probably could've done it herself if she put her mind to it.

"There. I got you... How're you feeling?" Dylan asked, combing the hair from her face.

"Tired." *Good* was what Hazel could've said, but surely that went without saying. She was achy and spent, and parts of her that hadn't even been touched seemed to thrum with exhaustion. "M'sorry," she slurred.

"For?"

"You didn't say —"

"I wanted you to come, sweetheart. That was so hot. You enjoyed it, right?"

Hazel tried to find the words — she really did — but her brain wouldn't cooperate.

Dylan didn't hold it against her. "Let's get you to bed."

Now Hazel understood the wisdom of having a bed so close to a torture chamber. She didn't know how she managed the twenty feet from ceiling hook to king-size mattress, but once she was horizontal, she was perfectly content to stay there. Dylan propped himself on his elbow beside her. "Are you cold?"

She shook her head.

"Thirsty?"

Hazel managed a crooked smile as she hugged the pillow to her chest. It smelled like Dylan's cologne. "What's with the Twenty Questions?"

"Comes with the territory." Dylan stroked her flank. "You won't have any bruises, but if you're sore right now, I can run you a bath…"

*You're way too coherent after that.* It took Hazel a moment to realize why. Bliss dimmed swiftly, replaced by guilt. Was she really so selfish?

She caught Dylan's hand in hers and used it as leverage to drag herself up. Aching limbs protested the attempt, but Hazel was all about mind over matter. She ignored Dylan's frown in favor of unbuckling his belt. By the time he caught on, she already had a hand down the front of his pants, into his boxers, curling around his erection. He was half hard, but he thickened even more in her fist, pre-cum slicking her thumb.

There was something incredibly gratifying about hearing his breath hitch. "What're you doing?"

"What does it look like?" Hazel licked her lips and, before she could think better of it, tugged him out of the confines of his slacks and pressed her lips to the silky cockhead.

Dylan swore under his breath. "Fuck, let me get a condom—"

Hazel wasn't listening. She hated the taste of latex in her mouth, anyway. A blow job wasn't even close to the top ten risks she'd taken today. She hollowed her cheeks around his shaft and sucked him deep. This part she remembered well. All it took was letting her throat relax, remembering to breathe through her nose, and soon her lips met her fingers at the base of his erection.

Dylan made a sound low in his throat, fisting her long hair, then bucked up. His body stiffened as he came.

Cum filled her mouth, seeping out of the corners of her lips.

She pulled back misty-eyed, but she knew not to cough until she'd let him slide out completely.

"Fuck, sorry. I thought you'd..." Dylan left off apologizing as she licked him clean, tremulous little moans creeping out of his throat as the aftershocks rode his spent body. He sank back into the mattress when Hazel shifted away. "That—that was unexpected."

"You're welcome," Hazel rasped out, her throat like sandpaper.

Dylan twisted around to glance at her, his eyes soft, lashes low over his cheeks.

"Thank you."

He looked debauched and edible, but Hazel was too exhausted to do much more besides loll in his bed and watch him. *Now* she could sit back, enjoy the afterglow.

"I should get cleaned up," Dylan mumbled after a beat. "Sure I can't tempt you with that bath?"

Hazel shook her head.

"Okay." He dragged himself up with some effort.

*A job well done.* That indefatigable voice at the back of her mind was up to its old tricks again. *Shame it's the first and last time...*

Hazel waited until the bathroom door had shut in Dylan's wake before staggering to her feet. She found her clothes and purse in the playroom. She tugged her dress on as best she could, forgoing underwear, girdle and tights and gritting her teeth when it came to pulling her shoes on.

She was combing her hair back into place when Dylan came out of the bathroom, sans pants, his untucked shirt hanging open over a pair of black boxers. His chiseled stomach briefly distracted Hazel from the wrinkle between his eyebrows.

"I should go," she said pre-emptively.

"Already?"

"I had a good time," Hazel replied, sidestepping the question. She got off. He got off. What more was there to do?

Dylan didn't seem to agree, but he nodded all the same. "Me too, it's just... Look, let me put some pants on, I'll drive you home."

"I called a cab." That was a lie, but Hazel had said far worse things to get out of sticky situations.

She could almost pretend she didn't care that Dylan's face fell in dismay or that a part of her badly, foolishly wanted to spend the night. That was one rule she couldn't afford to break. It was for the best.

"Are you sure?"

"Do I strike you as the kind of girl that needs handholding?" Hazel retorted, because she couldn't lie to his face after *that*.

"Okay," Dylan said, relenting. "You'll call me?"

"Sure."

"Hazel."

She was already halfway out of the bedroom, handbag slapping against her hip, when Dylan called her name. *Ask me to stay. Ask me to stay and I will.*

"Your dress is undone," Dylan said.

"Oh..." It took everything she had not to crumble when he came up behind her to do up the zipper. "Thanks."

"Any time."

She thought about pecking him on the cheek before she left, but in the end the fear of losing her resolve won out. The front door closed behind her with a dull clang as she took the steps on jelly legs.

Hands shaking, she called a cab from the lobby. The operator promised a fifteen minute wait, give or take. Hazel thanked him and hung up. Through the flimsy material of her dress, the stone step bit at the blood-hot welts on the backs of her thighs.

It was a relief when the overhead neon switched off at last, plunging her into pitch-black darkness.

# Chapter Seven

"What do you mean you're not coming in today?"

Hazel pinched the bridge of her nose between thumb and forefinger. "I'm not feeling too hot. Think it's something I ate…"

"Honey, do you need me to come over?" Sadie's tone veered from bewildered to concerned in an eye blink.

"No. I'll just sleep it off—"

"Christ," Sadie swore on the other end of the line.

"What?"

"Your boyfriend's here."

Hazel curled her tongue against the roof of her mouth. "Shit. I'm sorry…" She heard Marco shout for Sadie to get off the phone. She could only imagine the diner was full and tempers were running hot. Marco would be no happier once he heard she was taking the day off. "Look, don't tell him anything," Hazel pleaded, not quite sure which 'him' she meant.

Sadie gave no sign of having heard. "Or I could beat his ass with a tire iron. I know people. If he did something—"

"He was wonderful." *That's the problem.* 'Wonderful' hurt more when they left. "I'm serious, Sadie. It's all good. I just don't feel up to facing the world today."

"I'm coming over after work."

"You don't have to." It wasn't 'there's no need' because Hazel never wanted to be alone when she was down. Silence gave her thoughts room to roam. She'd grown up in a house that was quiet only at night. *And you left it for a reason.*

Sadie scoffed. "I'm coming over."

"Okay."

"Don't wallow. Whatever it is. If you're feeling up to it, go for a walk. Clear your head. Buy expensive shoes."

Hazel made no promises. She didn't want to give up the handy fiction of an upset stomach. It had served her well enough in high school.

She hung up and fell back into bed.

Sleep found her easily.

In her dreams, she went back to Dunby and the home she'd been so eager to flee. She found herself trying to get ready for school but finding all her clothes had disappeared. Her mother burst into the room to tell her she would be late.

A breath later, her father did the same. Then Buddy.

An endless succession of family and friends paraded before her bedroom door, all shrugging when she asked where her things were. And all along, pieces of her childhood haven vanished off the walls. It was an eternity before she noticed that every time her back was turned, her visitors removed another Backstreet Boys poster, another Missouri Princess Pageant trophy. She was down to her pink-swathed twin bed and an empty wardrobe by the time she jolted awake.

Rain pelted the window, fat droplets slamming against the pane like pebbles. It took Hazel a long moment to grasp that it wasn't the rain that had roused her.

Her cell vibrated on the bedside table, rocking the reading lamp and the stack of books balanced precariously on the corner. Hazel checked Caller ID.

*Dylan* gleamed on the screen.

"Duh…" He'd said he would wait for her call. This was proof of poor impulse control.

*Or maybe he just likes me?* Hazel dismissed the thought as she clicked Reject. He would call again later, when she was better prepared to face the conversation brewing on the horizon. Much like the tornadoes of her childhood, she knew she couldn't outrun it.

She endeavored to get back to sleep, but last night's events wouldn't give her peace. Sighing, Hazel kicked off the covers and stomped into her minuscule bathroom. Pipes rattled and clanged as water gushed from the shower spray.

It wasn't a matter of feeling dirty. True to his word, Dylan hadn't left any marks. Nothing hurt the day after he'd worked her over with a sure hand. Hazel leaned against the tiles. If she closed her eyes, she could see Dylan on his knees before her. She could feel the sting of the crop making the pleasure that much sweeter. Her clit throbbed with the memory, body yearning for touch despite the curl of shame in her belly. The shower ran cold before Hazel had exhausted the stock of lewd flashbacks. She wrapped herself in a towel and wrung out her hair before pinning it up in a messy twist.

Last night had been a happy accident—evidence that there were some good men left out there. So why did the woman staring back at her from the mirror look so hollow-eyed?

The phone shrilled in the other room.

It was Dylan. Again. This time, Hazel picked up.

"Hey..."

"Hey back. How are you feeling?" His voice sounded echo y, like he was speaking from inside a tunnel.

Was he asking because he'd stopped by the diner and she wasn't there or because of what they'd done last night? Hazel opted for the likelier option. "I'm not that much of a fixture that you can't digest breakfast at Marco's without seeing me, am I?" Never mind that she was still happy to pull double shifts—as long as they were in daylight—just so she wouldn't be cooped up at home, alone with her thoughts.

Dylan scoffed. "Sadie mentioned you weren't feeling well. Was it the salmon?"

"Salmon was fine."

"I thought so, too... But if you didn't like the salmon, I hope you know you can tell me. There are other dishes on the menu."

Hazel parked herself on the edge of the bed, chilly rivulets dripping from her hair down her spine. She smiled despite herself. "Or we could just eat in from now on. I do make a killer cheese casserole..."

"I wasn't really talking about salmon."

"I know." It wasn't the most obscure analogy he could've come up with. Her smile dimmed. "I don't know how to say this without coming across as giving you the brush-off."

"So don't say it," Dylan breathed, his voice dropping an octave.

"It's not fair to you."

"I don't want you to be fair. Be as—as unfair as you'd like, just... Give us a chance?"

Hazel ran her tongue along the flats of her teeth, mulling it over. She couldn't do that. Not only would it lead to heartache in the long run, but Dylan would regret ever talking her out of a quick and easy breakup. She knew how this story ended.

"Ward doesn't like me much, does he?" Hazel asked, trying another tack.

"Did he say that?"

"I thought it was implied." *Especially when he owned up to online stalking me to make sure I wasn't some kind of a gold-digger.* "Guess I can't blame him. I'd be protective, too, if I was your friends-with-benefits person." She'd nearly said 'guy', but more and more she was beginning to think homosexuality wasn't something that Dylan or Ward were comfortable admitting to. It made no difference.

They wouldn't be the first well-heeled men to take long walks across the Kinsey scale while keeping up a front of respectability.

Dylan was quiet for a long moment. "Could we talk over coffee?"

"Afraid someone bugged your phone?"

"No, but I can tell you've got some thoughts," Dylan said softly.

That was putting it mildly. Hazel glanced at the rain-spattered window. "You could come over."

"Right now?"

"Unless you're busy—"

"No," Dylan said, a little more forcefully than was necessary. "No, now is fine. I can come now."

"Bring coffee," Hazel told him.

She hung up and set about putting the apartment to rights. It wasn't as bad as it had been two nights ago, when they'd wound up at her place because his was under occupation. There were no dirty dishes and the living room was as spotless as it got. The bedroom was another matter. Hazel found last night's dress scattered at the foot of the bed, her pumps by the door. She stuffed her underclothes into the hamper with the rest of the laundry, to be washed in three days' time, the earliest she'd been able to book the washing machine in the basement.

Dylan rang the intercom just as she was brushing out the knots in her damp hair.

Hazel buzzed him in.

"I didn't know if you had breakfast already, so I got us a couple of BLTs," Dylan confessed, holding up a plastic bag.

"You're not huffing and puffing."

"They fixed the elevator." They stood in Hazel's foyer, neither of them entirely at ease, until Dylan sighed and leaned in to peck her on the cheek. "I'm sorry."

"What for?"

"Last night. This morning. Whatever's going on... I should've told Ward it was too soon, but he insisted."

Hazel felt her face heat. "Didn't seem like he knows how to take no for an answer."

She produced two plates and a couple of paper napkins from the kitchen before joining Dylan on the couch. The napkins were patterned with snowmen and mistletoe, remnants from last Christmas' sad-sack, one-woman feast—a far cry from three-figure dinners at an upscale restaurant in the heart of the city.

It was a little late to feel awkward around Dylan. After all, last night she'd been naked in his bed, his cock down her throat. Yoga pants and a hoodie couldn't be any more embarrassing than no clothes at all.

"Speaking of Ward," Dylan started cautiously, "I just got off the phone with him."

Hazel froze, paper cup halfway to her mouth. "Oh. Do you have report to him before you're allowed to see me?" She might have been able to keep the arch tone at bay if she'd bothered trying. "What did he say?"

"That he had a great time and would love it if we'd join him at his place in San Diego next time he decides he's too good for L.A... Full disclosure, I may have taken liberties with that last part."

"Huh." Hazel tilted into the cushions stacked against the armrest of the couch. "Didn't see that coming..." Intimidating, background-checking Ward wanted to play host. *What's he planning now? A 'greatest hits' exhibition?*

Dylan picked at a pill on his trouser leg. He was dressed for work, the clean lines of his suit a cross between undertaker and CIA operative. "I think you have it wrong."

"What, you mean Ward really, really likes me?" Hazel rolled her eyes. "He's not that good of an actor."

"No, but he does have a hard time making himself understood."

"His accent isn't *that* thick."

Dylan pressed his lips into a thin line, breathing out through his nose. He seemed to be trying hard to indulge her, but it was costing him. Hazel felt a touch of remorse for the unnecessarily flippant tone. When she got nervous, she lashed out whichever way she could.

"He's never been comfortable with new people. That's why he does his homework, why he overcompensates with a slew of anecdotes... It's not that he's trying to monopolize the conversation," Dylan insisted. "He's just nervous."

"He's a thirty-year-old CEO." Did it bear recalling? Hazel hadn't felt more out of her depth since she'd had to sit next to Reverend McDaniels at her brother's wedding, *after* the pictures came out.

"And in debt up to his neck. And trying to keep his father's company from sinking... If it's Ward you're worried about, don't be. He'll learn to like you."

"Or you'll what? Leave him?"

Dylan cocked his head. "Is that it, then? You're uncomfortable with our relationship."

It wasn't an accusation Hazel could easily refute. Instead, she scowled. "You're acting like I'm supposed to be okay dating a man who's sleeping with another dude. I don't know many women who'd be on board with that."

*And it's not why I'm struggling.* It would've been easier if she could have drawn a line in the sand and claim that she couldn't—wouldn't—step over it, come hell or high water. At least then she could pretend to have standards.

"I don't know any." Dylan set his plate on the coffee table and pushed himself up. It was too controlled to kindle panic in Hazel's gut.

He cut an incongruous picture, pacing the length of Hazel's living room in his Italian leather shoes, charcoal gray suit draping seamlessly down his body. It was a bit like hanging the Mona Lisa over an Ikea sideboard. It just didn't work.

"I've known Ward for more than a decade," he confessed. "And yes, there have been others since, but

I've never been interested in a relationship with any of them."

"Until I came along?" Hazel asked, arching her eyebrows.

Dylan abruptly stopped pacing, his back to the window. "Is that so hard to believe?"

"It's very flattering. Are you sure it's because you've never wanted to date anyone before and not that Ward wouldn't allow it?"

"Yes."

"That makes one of us," Hazel muttered under her breath. She knew that Dylan heard. She knew it in the narrowing of his eyes and the straightening of his broad shoulders, as if he was bracing for battle.

"Perhaps I didn't make myself clear," he replied, dipping into his 'Dom voice' at a moment's notice. "Ward Parrish is my closest friend. My relationship with him is not up for debate. If you're worried it'll interfere with what we have — don't be. I can keep them separate. I've done it for years."

All that kept Hazel from spitting her coffee back was some dormant sense of propriety and the knowledge that somewhere at the back of his mind, Dylan was probably judging her already. She barked out a mirthless laugh. "And if I'm not convinced, you'll pick him. Is that it?"

"I don't see it as a choice."

"Well, I do." It was Hazel's turn to stand. She pushed a slice of damp hair behind her ear. "I can't believe you're trying to guilt me for not wanting to share the man I'm seeing. Like that's an outrageous thing to ask!"

"It's not," Dylan agreed. "But it's not something I can offer."

"That settles it, I guess." It didn't feel like much of a victory. "I think you should go."

"Hazel—"

She shook her head. "Thanks for lunch."

Dylan didn't stop her turning her back on him. He didn't block her path as she started down the hall to the bedroom.

"I'll be in Shanghai for the next couple of weeks," he said to her retreating back. "Can I call you when I get back?"

*No* simmered on the tip of Hazel's tongue, rich and satisfying like chocolate liqueur. It was also the equivalent of closing a door she'd barely peeked through and too final to be spoken.

"It's a free country," Hazel retorted off-handedly.

The ugly wall-to-wall carpet in the living room and the dented linoleum that blanketed the entryway muffled Dylan's footfalls. The click of the door shutting in his wake rang like a bell toll.

By the time Hazel spun around, he was already gone.

# Chapter Eight

An hour stretched into three, then five. Noon rolled around before Hazel made herself pick at what was left of the BLTs. Her appetite remained elusive. No matter how faithfully she tried to devote herself to *Days of Our Lives* reruns, she couldn't stop replaying Dylan's parting shot in her head.

It spun in and out of focus like a screeching, broken record.

Hazel should have asked him to stay. She should've said *It's not you, it's me*. Clichés were cheap, but no cheaper than putting blame where there was none. She couldn't get over the chance that maybe some of what he'd said was true.

Maybe he did want her—and not just to smack around in bed.

She rose from the couch to dispose of the sandwich wrappers. The trashcan overflowed. She needed to take it down the curb, get at least one thing done for the day.

Anxiety bit at her insides. Sadie *had* recommended that she go for a walk.

*So why the makeup?*

Hazel blinked at her reflection, mindful of smearing the mascara she'd just applied.

*Why the push-up bra?*

She donned a black T-shirt and a pair of jeans. Sadie had returned her car keys the other day. Hazel grabbed them off the hook by the door—just in case she felt like going for a drive. According to sources, Mulholland was supposed to be quite the scenic route.

Garbage bag stowed in the appropriate dumpster, Hazel idled for a long beat on the curb. There was no harm in driving around. It might even help clear her head.

She kept up the illusion as she gunned the engine and peeled away from the sidewalk.

The Volvo shook when she changed gears, but otherwise lurched along smoothly. Hazel told herself that if the brakes stuck again, or if the dashboard gas gauge lit up, she'd turn back.

Driving around LA was Sadie's way of coping with a head full of terrible thoughts. Hazel preferred sleep—or work, when she absolutely couldn't get more of the former. But if she closed her eyes now, there was a good chance she'd be catapulted back to Dunby.

Or, worse, she'd dream herself back to college.

She didn't question her internal GPS when it bade her turn right on Aulden, or her foot when it eased off the gas. The odds of finding a parking spot were slim. Dylan and Ward were probably still at work.

Conviction didn't stop her keeping an eye out for a silver BMW or Dylan's eye-catching Tesla. She only saw the one. And lucky for her, Dylan had left a generous twenty feet between him and the next parked car.

Hazel slotted neatly into the gap, barely even grazing the curb with her rear tire.

*This is a bad idea.* She was better off going home and medicating with Ben & Jerry's.

She tore the keys out of the ignition before she could think better of it. Inside, the walk-up gleamed with flickering electric light, just as it had on her first visit. Hazel took the steps slowly, every footfall bringing her closer to the lip of an invisible ledge. She knuckled the doorbell with a mixture of dread and anticipation. Since she was here, she might as well.

It didn't mean that she was recanting.

It didn't mean—

Dylan wrenched open the sliding door, phone pressed to his ear. Confusion settled quickly on his features when he saw her on the landing.

"One moment, please..." He pressed the cell to his chest. "Hazel? What're you doing here?"

*I came to apologize. I came to ask you not to contact me again.* It was the first time in six years that Hazel found herself tongue-tied in a man's presence. Her courage threatening to slink away, she surged forward and pressed her lips to his.

It was a chaste kiss, but it might have been more if Dylan hadn't tilted back and out of her reach. "Let me call you back," he said into the phone. A moment later, he thumbed the Call End key and opened his door a little wider. "Think you'd better come in."

Hazel would've done it anyway, but the invitation raised goosebumps on her arms as she did so. The loft was different in the daytime. Amber light slanted through the west-facing windows, splashing across the floorboard in an artless, geometric array. Hazel noticed Dylan's suit jacket dangling from the back of a kitchen chair. She saw a laptop, lid open, on the table before it.

"Shouldn't you be at work?" was the closest thing to a *hello* to pass her lips.

Dylan shook his head, the picture of exhaustion, and bypassed the question. "I thought you didn't want to see me."

"Yes, well... I'm a woman. We're notoriously indecisive," she shot back, wincing.

Had that really come out of her mouth?

"That's not what I've found." Dylan crossed to the kitchen with a sure gait. He was so composed, so distant, that Hazel barely recognized him. "Would you like something to drink?"

She could put up with a lot—floggers, ropes—but she'd never mastered the cold shoulder. "I'm sorry," she blurted out, hating herself for caving in so easily. Hating Dylan for making her squirm while he pretended to peruse the contents of his fridge.

"What for?"

"Don't do that," Hazel pleaded. She didn't mean to make her voice small and pitiful. It just happened. Many things did. She was out of practice, hard limits blurred like smudged ink.

Dylan let the fridge door click shut.

"Don't make me grovel," Hazel clarified. "I can't... I'm not good at it and if you pull that shit again, I'll walk out."

"Are there only two speeds with you?"

"What?"

Dylan propped his elbows against the kitchen island, granite dark and gritty against his impeccable white sleeves. "Either you cut and run, or you throw yourself in full throttle? Seems like a dangerous way to live."

"Spare me the pop psychology."

He tightened his jaw. "Why are you here, Hazel?" There it was, that gravelly note in his voice, the suggestion of authority where he had none.

"I told you—"

"You said something about apologizing. Were that true, you wouldn't be trying so hard to pick a fight."

Hazel couldn't have answered if he stayed put, scrutinizing her from across the room. It was a foregone conclusion as he approached. She sucked in a breath when he slid his fingers through her hair. He had such beautiful hands. They hurt so good when he used them to strike, to pinch—to pull. Hazel smothered a whimper as the caress became a vicious tug, Dylan's way of holding her still.

"What do you need?" he asked, pressing in so close that when he spoke, his breath fanned against her lips.

It was as irrational as it was pathetic, but Hazel wanted nothing more than to drown in his scent. "Hurt me," she pleaded, as she hadn't in years. *Hurt me. It'll make you feel better.*

*You'll forgive me then.*

Dylan released her abruptly, eyes dark with promise. "Are you sure?"

"Yes."

His gaze darted over her face, taking in the set line of her jaw, the furrow between her brows. Then he nodded, rallying.

"I want you naked and spread over the spanking bench. Go."

Hazel's feet knew the way. She was tugging off her shirt before she reached the bedroom door. Dylan struck her as the fastidious type, so she made sure to fold her clothes into a neat pile before entering the playroom. Her heart slammed against her ribcage as the lights flicked on. *Motion sensors.* She scoped the torture implements on the walls. Dylan had invested an arm and a leg in this little corner of hell. *But is it his money or Ward's?*

She had a brief, stomach-churning thought that she should check for cameras before she did anything else, but the echo of familiar footfalls aborted the intention.

The spanking horse was small and padded, with a couple of welded strap loops on the underside. Hazel positioned herself with her back to the door—and waited.

Dylan's tread aborted a good fifteen feet away from the spanking horse, the silence pregnant with foreboding. She tried to see herself through his eyes— pale and shivering, her hands awkwardly clasped under the padded bench. She'd rested her knees right up against the legs, but she parted them when Dylan crossed to her and nudged the toes of his leather shoe against her calves.

"You've done this before."

It wasn't a question, but Hazel breathed out a "Yes" all the same.

"With?"

"A switch or a paddle." *Or your bare hand.* Her experience ran the gamut from impromptu fun to aches so persistent she couldn't sit down for days.

Dylan brushed her hair from her shoulder, ignoring her shiver. "That's not what I meant."

"Oh... *Oh.*" Was she supposed to tell him about that? The rules, as she remembered them, were very clear. Keeping secrets from her Dom was a no-no. But Dylan wasn't that in any real capacity, not yet, and Hazel found herself prevaricating. "Someone else, a while ago..."

"A boyfriend?"

*No.* "Yes." *Sort of.* The more she talked, the less sure of herself she felt.

She heard more than saw Dylan crouch down. He slid a knuckle under her chin. The camber of her neck was only uncomfortable for an instant. Then Dylan was kissing her and Hazel felt something inside her — a tense knot of dread and suspicion — promptly unravel.

"Drop your head," he instructed, guiding her with a warm palm on her nape. He didn't sound angry anymore. He wasn't asking questions she couldn't answer.

Hazel did as told, cheeks burning when the spanking bench creaked beneath her weight. She gripped her wrists a little tighter. Dylan wouldn't keep shoddy equipment in his playroom, would he? He wouldn't put her in danger just for kicks.

*His usual submissives are probably not as heavy...*

That small, treacherous voice at the back of her mind abruptly fell silent as the sound of skin hitting skin rang out like a party popper. A sharp sting followed quickly on its heels, heat rushing up the length of Hazel's spine to explode behind her eyes. She gasped. Until that moment, she hadn't considered how much it might hurt to make herself into Dylan's willing victim. The end — squaring things between them so he didn't drop her before she was ready — more than excused the unorthodox means.

It also sparked a flare of arousal in the pit of her stomach.

Through the roar of blood in her ears, Hazel discerned the sound of Dylan's voice. "Think you can take a dozen?"

"Yeah." She swallowed hard, pushing past a quiver of doubt. "Yes."

Dylan stroked the hurt from her flesh before raising his hand again. The second swat caught her across the right cheek, a mere glancing blow that nevertheless kindled a low, throbbing ache in her backside. Her cunt clenched with the third slap. Her hands began to sweat by the half-dozen.

"Beautiful," Dylan murmured, as though to himself, and Hazel resolved to suffer the next six strokes.

She curled her toes into the stone, bracing herself. Swat number eight slid her forward about half an inch, her nipples dragging against the sleek leather. She squared her shoulders to keep it from happening again. No matter how pleasurable, she wasn't supposed to enjoy punishment without Dylan's say-so.

By ten, Hazel couldn't slow her breaths, much less her racing thoughts. Dylan slid his fingers down, past her tailbone, and the air in her lungs evaporated promptly.

"Have you done this, too?" he asked conversationally. The deliberate stroke of a fingertip against her asshole brought up memories.

"Yes," Hazel bit out, when what she meant was *Do I look like a virgin to you?*

She couldn't play the innocent when he slid a finger into her cunt. She was too wet, too desperate for him. Her body always gave her away, even when cameras flashed in the dark.

*Look at me, baby…*

Hazel bucked against the spanking horse, wooden legs scraping the floor. She threw off Dylan's purposeful strokes before he could touch her clit.

He chuckled. "Where do you think you're going?"

The pull of fingers through her hair was enough to recall her to order. *Fuck.* "Sorry—sorry, I didn't. You took me by surprise." Hazel chanced a glance over her shoulder, face hot. "You-you said twelve?"

She had two more blows to go before her sins were absolved.

"Keeping count, were you?"

Wasn't she supposed to? Hazel mulled over her answer, but before she could speak, Dylan had already pulled back his hand. He finished off with a series of sharp, cracking slaps, her backside shaking with the force of each one.

Hazel lurched forward, hugging the bench to her chest. She could barely breathe between blows, searing pain rushing across her flesh, turning her inside out. She used to be stronger than that. She used to take closer to forty strokes without a peep. Now, though...

Dylan breezed past twelve in a frenzy. Hazel's breaths came a little louder with each ensuing strike, forcibly tearing free of her lungs, no matter how she tried to silence them.

"Say mercy when you can't take any more—"

"Mercy!" she choked out. "Mercy, please, please..." A smothered cry tangled in her throat as Dylan ran his feverish palm over her cheeks.

"When I want you keeping count, I'll tell you," Dylan said as he reached between her legs and slid two fingers into her throbbing pussy.

Hazel trembled, inner muscles clenching at the sudden intrusion, but she was so turned on, so ready for him that there was no burning stretch. No discomfort. If he wanted to hurt her, Dylan would have to use something a lot bigger than his fingers. She nearly told him as much.

"Look at you," he murmured, "sopping wet... You got off on that, didn't you?"

"Yeah."

Dylan could have left it at that, but clearly he was a sadist at heart, so he didn't. "Is that what you came here for? You wanted me to take my frustrations out on you so you'd feel better?"

A small, guilty part of Hazel wanted to protest that charge. She had come to make things right. There was a world of difference between trying to fix things and using Dylan to scratch an itch. She'd never do that.

*Wouldn't you?* taunted that small inner voice. *You always were manipulative.*

"Open your mouth," Dylan ordered. A half second later, slick fingers were pressed to her lips and Hazel had a short-lived choice between obeying and having the evidence of her arousal smeared over her lips and chin.

It wasn't a choice at all—humiliation had never been her kink.

She rolled her tongue around his digits and hollowed her cheeks. She wasn't ashamed to taste herself. She'd done it before Dylan, before college. If Dylan wanted her to mimic fellating his cock, then she could do that, too. She wanted to please him so badly.

"Fuck," he exhaled, low and heartfelt. "You don't know how sexy you look right now..."

*Take a picture. It'll last longer.*

Hazel tore her mouth away and pressed her cheek to the spanking horse. Remorse shot through her, even though she hadn't spoken out loud. "Can... Can I get up now?"

"Do you want to?"

He had no right to ask or to sound so tender when he did. That wasn't how this worked. Past the submissive pose and the ache in her backside, Hazel wouldn't have been on her knees if she didn't want to cede the making of decisions to him.

She mulled over the question. "Do you want me to?"

"What do you think?"

Heat crawled to her face, two parts frustration to one part anxiety. How was she supposed to answer that? What could she say to make Dylan understand that she didn't know and she wasn't—

Her answer must have been too long in coming, because Dylan rose and shifted out of her field of vision with a few broad steps.

Panic rippled down Hazel's spine, her hackles only soothed once she felt him settle between her legs. She registered each individual click of the metal zipper, each rustle of cloth and plastic-y tear and knew what was coming. It didn't stop breath from slamming out of her lungs as Dylan ran the tip of his erection along her inner folds.

"What are you thinking, Hazel?" He sounded ragged, as if it was taking everything he had not to press inside.

"I—I don't know."

"Yes, you do. Don't play coy. Tell me what you're thinking. Do you want this?"

She didn't need to think about that. Her sopping pussy should've clued him in. "Yeah. God, yeah, please…"

"How?"

The litany of pleas brimming on the tip of her tongue came to a screeching halt. Of course Dylan wouldn't want her begging. That would've been too easy.

"However you want, Sir—"

She thought she heard Dylan suck in a breath at the stray honorific, but before she could figure out if he was pleased or enraged, he pulled away. No, not just away. His shoes clicked as he stepped back, the distance between them widening by the second.

Hazel twisted around at the waist. "Wait, no... What did I do?" Hot tears brimmed in her eyes. She struggled to blink them away. "Dylan, come back. I'm sorry—"

"Hey, hey... You're okay. Look at me." Dylan caught her by the shoulders, brushing his thumb across her cheek. "Hazel, stop."

She heard the order and clamped down on the raging, aching bruise inside her. She raised her gaze to his. "I'm a hot mess."

"Do you need a break?"

"No, just—tell me what I did wrong?" She reasoned that it was safe to ask now that Dylan was with her, holding her.

He pressed a kiss to her temple. "Nothing. Here. Do you want to sit—?"

Hazel shook her head, resisting when he made to pull her up. The underfloor heating made it comfortable to stay where she was. "What did you want to hear?"

"An answer—a *real* answer would have been nice," Dylan said, smiling crookedly. "Sorry. I didn't mean to make you freak out."

*You think* that *was a freak-out?* Hazel blew out a throaty laugh. "Don't flatter yourself."

Dylan wasn't so easily persuaded. "Sure you don't want to take a break?"

"I want to do this—with you." She slid a hand over his thigh, the soft wool of his slacks bunching up beneath her fingers. "Please?"

He considered the request for a long beat, the wrinkle between his eyebrows spelling out his hesitation. As soon as he raised his gaze to hers, Hazel knew she'd won.

"Straight answers from now on."

She nodded, already slipping back into the familiar routine of command and compliance. The tight pull of Dylan's hand in her hair helped in that regard. She went down a little deeper, tucking her heels and settling her racing heartbeat. It felt good to stop fighting.

Dylan gave her a few breaths to get herself under control, then tugged her to her feet. This time she went, rocking a little on wobbly legs.

"On the swing."

It was a welcome directive. Hazel oriented herself toward the steel frame nailed into the floor and gripped the metal chains on either side. A broad strip of leather drooped loosely from the frame. It swayed as she turned and gingerly dropped her weight back. She tamped down a flash of worry at the thought of bringing the whole contraption down beneath her.

Dylan was waiting. She'd delayed long enough.

The leather chains clicked with every twist and wriggle. Hazel anchored her hands into the two that stretched above her head. Her heart was pounding, a syncopated rhythm that had less to do with fear than anticipation. It got louder when Dylan took hold of her ankle and slid her foot through a leather strap.

There were no cuffs, but Hazel didn't need to be tied down to feel trapped. She flexed her toes.

"Cramp?" Dylan dug his thumbs into the balls of her feet before she could shake her head. It felt good.

*Christ, he could pick lint off my shoulder and I'd probably go weak in the knees.*

If Dylan noticed, he was too good at this to let it show. He walked his fingertips over her bare legs, around the leather straps and down, along her quivering inner thighs. Hazel sucked in a breath as he grazed her labia with his thumbs. Not stroking, not slapping — which she knew she shouldn't have wished for but did anyway — just tracing her slick folds while expectation mounted in her breast.

Hazel sucked her lips between her teeth to smother a plea for more, for faster. Her cheeks flamed. If he didn't do something soon, there was a good chance she'd come like this, untouched, every inch of her exposed to his greedy eyes. Much as she wanted an orgasm, it wouldn't feel right. She wanted more.

Dylan traced her pussy with a fingertip before entering her in one smooth, delicious press.

"Fuck..." Hazel threw her head back, chains clinking around her as the swing swayed back and forth. Her inner muscles clenched, grasping at him as he made to withdraw.

"You're so tight," she heard him murmur. "Been a while, has it?"

Hazel didn't want to admit it, but Dylan had asked her for straight answers. She nodded hastily.

"Don't worry," Dylan growled, "I won't go easy on you."

He lent action to words a moment later, making short work of the fastenings on his slacks and sliding on a condom. Hazel's addled brain snagged on that flimsy detail. An objection that rose up in her throat — *I'm on the pill. It's okay* — thoughts spiraling from one end of the spectrum to the other. But this wasn't about thinking or offering input.

*You're his submissive. You don't demur.*

Dylan seized her hip in a sure hand, as though in reminder. He didn't pound into her — *that* would've hurt, and probably not in a good way — but he gave her little to no time to adjust to the steady pressure of his cock inside her before withdrawing and entering her again.

He set a punishing pace, control unflagging even as the tendons in his neck pulled taut.

For all that Hazel tried to anchor herself, the swing offered no purchase. She swayed back and forth at his urging, the slick, vulgar echo of skin on skin soft at first, but rapidly gaining in volume. Dylan was merciless. He stayed inside her after the first few dozen thrusts, barely letting her slip away more than an inch before pulling her down again. There would be bruises where he gripped her waist so tightly, Hazel was sure, and red welts where her abused backside scraped the leather swing. It was a delicious sort of pain—the kind that grounded her.

The kind she wanted more of.

Dylan must have sensed it. He grabbed her throat as he buried himself inside her on a particularly arduous thrust. Hazel cried out. She was a long way from choking, but that didn't make her feel any less aroused at the possibility. Dylan could squeeze down at a moment's notice. If the fancy took him, he could have her thrashing, blue in the face, gasping, gasping—

Climax slammed into her without warning, a wave of pleasure racing down her hips and thighs to pool into her toes, then bouncing back up, vibrating tight behind her pulsing clit. Her legs jerked in the straps, body practically jackknifing in the sling. The clutch of her inner muscles squeezed Dylan tight as his rhythm fell apart.

Within a handful of ragged thrusts, he came, too, grunting through his orgasm as Hazel whimpered, pitiful in his grasp.

It wasn't until she felt him palm her cheek that she noticed he'd fucked her to the brink of tears. His face swam above her, features blurry around the edges.

"You okay?"

He sounded so concerned. Hazel nodded and turned her head to press a kiss to the crease of his lifeline. Her hands ached from gripping the chains for dear life, her hips were bruised and she was sure to be sore tomorrow, but none of those things mattered. She felt more relaxed than she had in a long time. She was better than okay.

She'd made it through the scene without falling apart.

# Chapter Nine

The bathroom door opened smoothly, a cloud of steam rushing out as Dylan emerged with a towel wrapped around his waist.

"I could get used to that view," Hazel teased from the bed. She scooted a little to the center of the mattress in silent invitation.

"It's certainly doing wonders for my ego." Dylan crawled up beside her, his chest warm and shower damp where it brushed her arm. "How are you feeling?"

*Too soon to tell. My freak-outs need time to marinate.*

"Good." It was close enough to the truth. She craned her neck, tangled hair spilling across the pillow as she glanced up at Dylan. His smooth-shaven cheeks were dark with a rosy flush. She couldn't help but feel gratified to notice that he had a hard time *not* staring at her naked body. "Is this the part where you debrief me like a good Dominant?"

"How predictable you make me sound!"

"I don't mind predictable..." She certainly hadn't minded when she was clutching the spanking horse to her chest or swinging back and forth while Dylan rutted against her. Nothing about that had been concrete in her mind's eye when she had rung his doorbell, but she was pleased with how everything had turned out.

Dylan cupped her breast with a gentle hand, stroking his thumb over her nipple as if to say *Predictable enough for you?* A tremor rippled across Hazel's flesh. Afterglow was often pitted with little bursts of startled pleasure, but she'd never been the type to push past exhaustion unless she absolutely had to.

"You didn't tell me that you'd done this before last night," Dylan noted, shaking her from the fog of tactile pleasure.

"You didn't ask."

Dylan met her gaze. "We don't have to talk about it if it's painful. I was just curious..."

*Of course you were. You and Ward are all about poking sleeping dogs.*

"There's not much to talk about," Hazel retorted. This time, it was a bald-faced lie. It was also the lesser of two evils. She didn't want to invite that part of her past into her present, much less inform Dylan of her neuroses when he was just beginning to warm to her.

"Was he your first Dom?" Dylan prodded gently.

"Was Ward yours?" It wasn't what she'd meant to ask, but she couldn't deny wanting to know. Ward's hold on Dylan confused as much as it annoyed her. Envy might have played a part, too.

Dylan's expression shuttered, but he didn't pull away. "He was," he admitted.

"And now?" *Give an inch...*

"And now—" Dylan sighed. "He's my friend."

Hazel wanted to ask for details — the why and how of it — but she could feel Dylan becoming closed off and grim beside her, so she changed the subject. "He was a pretty good teacher. You're good at this."

"Yeah?" The rueful tilt to Dylan's lips made all the hoop jumping worthwhile.

"Very good. You're *Thank heavens I don't have a desk job* good."

"Always with the ego stroking…" Dylan dug a knuckle into her flank. Hazel squirmed, but she could read no heat into the rebuke. "You're good, too," he said. "Even if… Would I be correct in guessing it's been a while?"

Hazel nodded, although it should've been obvious. "I'm out of practice, I know. If you just give me a chance —"

Dylan shushed her with a kiss. When he pulled away, he was grinning, eyes bright and giddy. "I intend to give you all the chances you want."

"Right, because practice makes perfect."

Scoffing, Dylan traced the dip in her chin with his thumb. "Not just that. I like you."

Hazel's heart slowly dropped back into the cage of her ribs, making it easy to breathe again. She thought about telling him about the time she fell off Buddy's bike into a wooden fence, about blood gushing over her chin like a font and everyone treating her like she'd gotten what she deserved. She thought about Dylan holding her in thrall like this, night after night, until they tired of each other.

In the end, she made do with returning the smile, some complicated, fanciful muscle pulling back flips in her chest.

\* \* \* \*

Dylan asked her to spend the night, but his flight was at six in the morning and Hazel didn't want to be around for the long, drawn-out goodbyes. "Keeping me up all night isn't goodbye," Dylan countered with a dazzling, indolent smile.

She caught his hand before he could reach beneath the covers and cup her sex. His touch was electric. Hazel didn't fool herself into thinking she could resist him for long.

"Some of us have to work in the morning."

The drudgery of a morning shift aside, she didn't want to be there when Ward finally crawled out of his room — if he was even at the loft — or came back home, if he was not. She'd sooner avoid seeing him again altogether if she could help it. Ward Parrish was the timer on the bomb. The more time she spent fiddling with the wires, the more likely it was that the block of TNT would detonate.

Dylan insisted on seeing her off. He walked her down to the car in a pair of loose-fitting sleep pants and a thin T-shirt. Hazel let him press her into the hood of the Volvo and kiss her with icy lips. The once familiar lilt of cicadas was absent in the over-paved, concrete-everywhere suburbs that had enveloped Aulden Way. The night seemed to be holding its breath.

"Go back inside before you catch your death…"

"I'm fine where I am," he murmured against her lips.

"Really? Because I'm pretty sure I'm feeling some shrinkage."

His laugh was warm and generous, and Hazel told herself that it was genuine, too. She'd never been very good at spotting liars.

Dylan pecked her on the cheek before he withdrew, hugging his sides.

"You're not going to do that thing where you stand on the curb and watch me drive off, are you?" Hazel wanted to know.

He shook his head, grinning. "Absolutely not."

"Because that would be lame."

"Totally lame," he agreed.

Hazel got behind the wheel and clicked the door shut. It took a couple of tries to get the key into the ignition. Her fingers felt big and clumsy, a side effect of wallowing in bed for the better part of two hours. She had to concentrate to gun the engine. The Volvo sputtered a couple of times before roaring to life. Dylan was still on the sidewalk when she glanced up, rocking on his heels.

"It's just two weeks, right?" Hazel asked, then repeated the question once she'd rolled down the window. She had to pitch her voice over the rumble of the car to make herself heard.

Even then, it was touch and go enough for Dylan to rest both elbows on the door and duck his head inside. "What?"

"It's two weeks."

"Until?"

Hazel cocked an eyebrow. "You come back?"

"Oh. I thought you meant until the next time you let me warm your ass with a paddle."

A tingle raced down her spine at the hungry cadence in his voice. She flexed her hands around the steering wheel. "We'll see."

Dylan slid a finger under her chin and made her look at him. Hazel didn't take much prompting. She yearned for the brush of his lips against hers even as she still felt the imprint of his kisses buried deep beneath her flesh.

He didn't oblige this time. "Two weeks," he said, "then you're *all* mine." He pulled back before Hazel could come up with a clever retort. The chassis vibrated with the thump of his palms. "Drive safe, okay?"

"Okay." Hazel put the Volvo in gear and slowly eased out of the parking space. She tried to resist glancing in the rearview mirror, but temptation won out.

Sure enough, Dylan stood on the curb, hugging his sides and shivering in his weather-inappropriate attire. His reflection diminished with every asphalt-scraping roll of the tires, but his presence lingered inside the car like a specter.

When she was far enough to be sure that Dylan wouldn't see it, Hazel allowed herself a sigh of relief. She took a left at the first intersection and let Dylan disappear from her sights. Two weeks was nothing, a mere drop in the bucket. Per experience, it was also more than enough time to forget and be forgotten.

The sodium street lights cast dull shadows over the Volvo, washing out the angry red in Hazel's cheeks and obscuring the bone-white pallor of her fingers around the steering wheel. She was supposed to be good at cutting and running. She had done it before.

What was so different about Dylan?

The answer was simple. *Nothing. Absolutely nothing.*

\* \* \* \*

The first day after Dylan flew off, Hazel sped through her morning shift like an automaton. She was so efficient getting orders in and out of the kitchen and refilling glasses of Diet Coke that Marco even asked if she was on drugs. She spent the hours after her shift cleaning up her apartment.

She hadn't realized how cluttered it had gotten until she'd spent a few hours at the loft. She channeled her simmering anxiety into scrubbing dinner plates with various bits of takeout still stuck to them and separating her laundry. She vacuumed every square inch of the floor—which wasn't hard to do, considering how small her apartment was—and washed the windows. And when she was finished with that, she took up reorganizing the inside of her wardrobe.

Hazel survived the first day with nary a thought about Dylan.

It got worse as the week wore on.

One evening as she was waiting for her shift to start, the diner almost empty around her, the hubbub in her head got so bad that Hazel found herself dialing the one number she'd never been able to forget.

Her mother picked up on the second ring. "Hazel? What's wrong?"

They traded that question back and forth every time they called each other on something other than a holiday.

"Nothing. Everything's good. I was just…wondering how you were. Over there." Hazel ran her fingernail through the scuff marks on the wall. A suspicious stain marred the plaster about two feet from the floor. Hazel decided to stop touching dubiously clean surfaces. "How's Buddy?"

"All right…"

The squeak of hinges echoed down the line. Hazel pictured her mother stepping out of the kitchen, past the screen door, and onto the porch.

The Midwest was two hours ahead. It was a miracle Mrs. Whitley was still awake.

"And Rhonda?" Hazel pressed.

"She's all right, too... The baby's coming any day now."

Hazel heard the question in her mother's voice. *Will you fly down for the christening?* She spoke before it could be asked. "Bet Rhonda can't wait."

"Oh, she's been great. Reminds me of when I was pregnant with Buddy..." The story was a staple of their family life, dredged up every May fifth, along with streamers and fireworks, and the mountain of presents Buddy never solicited. "You, on the other hand!" Hazel's mother hummed. "Just goes to show, I suppose..."

"Guess so," Hazel echoed. *I was a troublemaker before I was even born. Ain't that nice to hear?* She twirled the telephone cord around her finger, watching the skin go from pale to dark brown. "Were they very pissed off at me...you know, for missing out on the shower?" She said 'they' but what she really meant was Rhonda.

Perfect Rhonda who was a delight even when she was pregnant, whom everybody loved.

Hazel desperately wanted to hate her. She had a feeling that it would be easier to stomach than simply not being liked by her.

Her mother was silent too long to be honest. "They understood."

*Because you explained it to them.*

"Good."

"I have to go, Hazel. It's late."

"Oh, right." Hazel swayed back and forth on her heels. "Don't let the bedbugs bite."

"I'll tell your father you said hi."

"Sure.

There was nothing more to say after that and yet Hazel still felt a pang of hurt when the line went dead. *Who knew? You can't medicate one ache by setting yourself up for another.* Hazel promised herself she wouldn't call her mother again, no matter how loudly the thought of Dylan clamored in her head. No matter how lonely she felt.

Work was there to distract her—and when that failed, she had Sadie.

# Chapter Ten

It had been a bad idea when Sadie first insisted and it became an even worse one when she wouldn't let Hazel weasel out.

"You have to come," she had wheedled again that afternoon. "You're turning into your mother right before my eyes and I will *not* let that happen."

Maybe it was the dreaded M word or maybe it was a matter of feeling lonely after a few days with not even an unwanted visitor to spoil her routine. Regardless, a week into Dylan's business trip, Hazel allowed Sadie to drag her out of the house under the pretext of drinks and loud music—and more, if Sadie got her way.

The real objective of the outing became clearer once Med School Frank showed up. He painted a quiet, unobtrusive picture at Sadie's elbow, never straying farther than an inch or two at a time. The strobe lights reflected in his glasses.

"What about him?" Sadie asked, shouting to make herself heard over the music.

Hazel tracked her gaze to a handsome brunet grinding between a couple of likewise stunning women. They had freaky one-night stand with awkward walk of shame written all over them.

"Think he's taken."

"Well, keep looking!"

Med School Frank shot Hazel a pitying smile. He and Sadie had just passed the two-month mark. Sadie seemed to have settled into the relationship—inasmuch as Sadie settled into anything. She constantly name dropped Frank into conversations with Marco. She texted him every hour, only to then gush about his latest quip to Hazel. More and more when she asked Hazel out for a drink after work, it was a given that Frank would be joining them.

It was lucky he improved on acquaintance, Hazel mused, leaning her elbows on the bar and tilting her gaze away from the numerous hot, nubile bodies bumping and grinding on the dance floor. She wasn't in the mood to join them.

"How's tricks, Frank? Classes going okay?"

"Mostly labs now," he answered, nodding. He seemed as out of his element in the club as Hazel felt, but he wasn't the one meant to be on the hunt for a rebound.

Sadie elbowed her in the ribs. "Oh, what about the cute one over there? I think he's making eyes at you."

Hazel reluctantly followed her gaze to a skinny Romeo with black-framed glasses and spiky, gelled hair. Improbably, he was indeed looking at Hazel.

Her cheeks began to heat as he flagged down the bartender. He definitely pointed toward Hazel. The bartender nodded. It took a matter of seconds to assemble a Cosmopolitan, which he brought over to Hazel's end of the bar.

"For you," the bartender said, and set the Martini glass on the bar in front of Sadie. "From a secret admirer."

At the other end of the bar, Romeo smiled coyly.

Hazel laughed. Her stomach had dropped like an actual stone, burrowing somewhere deep in the basement of the club, where not even the dull thumping rhythm of the music could reach it. "Oh, man. I should've seen that coming."

"I'm *so* sorry..." Sadie made a face at the bartender, mortified. "You can take this back. I'm not... I don't want it."

The bartender stared like she'd grown a second head, reacting only when Frank curled a proprietary arm around Sadie's waist

"Oh, I'll have it," Hazel said, rolling her eyes. "It's paid for, right?" She raised the glass in toast to Sadie's secret admirer, whose cheeks had begun to tint a winsome shade of pink. "Free booze is free booze."

Sadie smiled weakly. "I'm sorry..."

Hazel waved a hand. "Forget about it." She took a sip of the cocktail. It tasted of the lies brimming on her tongue. "You know what? On second thought, I think I *am* going to dance. Watch my drink." Cranberry juice sloshed up to the rim and threatened to spill over the lip of the Martini glass.

She turned away before Sadie's pained expression could graft itself any deeper under her skin. This wasn't the first time they'd gone out together and men had noticed Sadie first—or at all—while ignoring Hazel. It also wasn't the first time Sadie had actively tried to find her a dance partner only to discover that there were no willing candidates.

Dunby High had set the tone when they were kids. Everything since was simply predestined.

Hazel brushed her fingertips under her eyes as surreptitiously as she could, nodding along to music played too loud for her ears to distinguish anything more than pounding drums and a sweeping, electric hum. She fervently hoped that her makeup wasn't running. It would add another layer of cheerlessness to the evening—more so than the awkward, partnerless bobbing Hazel was doing as she wove deeper and deeper into the throng.

When she looked back, she couldn't see the bar or Sadie's blonde hair—done up in a Princess Leia inspired do for the evening.

She startled when someone sidled up behind her, whirling around to find a smarmy stranger grinning as he thrust his hips in her general direction. Hazel wondered if this was the kind of rebound Sadie had in mind when she decreed that they needed to get her laid. Lothario over there had two arms, two legs, presumably a working dick. He cleared the threshold of desperation.

"No, thanks," Hazel shouted over the music.

The guy mimed 'what?' with a flick of his wrists, still approaching. He was bigger than Hazel by about a head, his shoulders testing the too-small muscle shirt he'd donned for the evening.

Before Hazel could extricate herself, he wound an arm around her waist and pulled her into his lap, grinding into her backside with his denim-clad dick.

Hazel went rigid, a hot flash rushing to her cheeks, turning the inside of her mouth to arid desert and her fists to useless lumps of coal.

A camera flash lit up the dark with the stop-start of strobe lights. *Just for us, baby…*

The vision rose out of the depths of memory, adrenaline spiking in her veins.

"Get the fuck away from me!" Hazel shoved as hard as she could, sending the guy teetering back into another couple. The woman shouted, affronted, and the man shoved back.

Hazel's personal Lothario only had eyes for her. He drew himself up, glowering, and made to take a step forward, into easy reach of her fist.

"No need for that," Hazel heard, just before someone caught her forearm.

She spun around, ready to face Moron Number Two, and her jaw just about dropped. "What're *you* doing here?"

Ward didn't get the chance to answer. Lothario covered the distance between them with a couple of broad strides. "You'd best tell your woman that if she raises a hand, she better be ready to —"

The tail end of his boast was lost to a poorly telegraphed right hook that nevertheless caught him right in the jaw.

Ward shook out his wrist, wincing. "Fuck, that hurt…"

"Have you lost your fucking mind?" Hazel cried out. A few heads had turned, but most people seemed intent on turning a blind eye to the fool crawling around the floor of the club.

Hazel pushed Ward back, marching him away from the scene of the crime. If Lothario had some buddies with him, their best bet was an ice bucket and a broad number of witnesses, neither of which could be found outside the club.

Ward let her bully him as far as the bar, where he dropped sullenly onto a stool. "You're welcome."

Hazel ignored him in favor of scanning their immediate vicinity for signs of Sadie and Frank. They were nowhere to be seen. Probably dancing, Hazel reasoned, which was just as well. She didn't want to have to explain Ward or the grabby asshole.

"Let me see," she ordered, pulling Ward's hand away from his reddened knuckles. His thumb was already swelling with a purplish bruise. "Jesus, did you hit him with a closed fist?"

"Really? You're going to criticize my technique?" Ward scoffed. "That'll teach me to come to your aid…"

"I didn't *need* your help. I had it under control."

Ward rolled his eyes. "He was a head bigger than you."

"So?" Hazel lifted herself up with a hand on the bar and propped a knee on the stool to scoop ice out of a nearby bucket. The bartender called out an objecting note. Hazel ignored him. "Here, hold this."

"You can't do that," the tender griped, furrowing his pierced eyebrows. "This isn't a self-service—"

"Would you rather I call the cops?" Hazel shot back.

"Excuse her," Ward scoffed. "She's a little high-strung. Ow!"

Hazel smiled through clenched teeth and closed his abused fist around the fast-melting ice cubes. "Look who's talking."

Ward didn't heed her. "I'll have a whiskey," he said, sliding a twenty across the bar, "and your discretion."

The bartender shook his head and he snagged the crisp bill. He walked away muttering under his breath about a lover's tiff.

Beneath his makeshift compress, Ward flexed his fingers weakly. "Aren't you all Florence Nightingale? You can give it a rest, you know. He's not here."

Hazel didn't have to ask who Ward was referring to. She withdrew her hands from his chilled fingers, annoyance sparking in her gut. "I know he's not here.

He's in Shanghai, right? Business trip or something..." *You're not the only one he talks to, jerk.* Then again, she wouldn't have been surprised if Dylan had come back early and failed to share the good news. They didn't have that kind of relationship.

They didn't have much of a relationship at all. Hazel banished the thought.

Ward's expression remained pinched and oddly quizzical.

"He didn't tell you."

"What?" It shouldn't have surprised her to discover that Dylan had more secrets. He compartmentalized well. Hazel was a rank amateur by comparison.

"He went to see his birth parents."

Hazel cocked an eyebrow. "If he didn't tell me, then I'm not supposed to know." She meant it as a rebuff. She didn't need him to funnel intelligence. She didn't need him widening the chasm she'd already started digging between herself and Dylan.

"He didn't tell *me* not to tell you," Ward defended, pedantic. He exchanged the melting ice cubes for the whiskey. Hazel saw herself reflected in the fast-growing puddle on the counter. She should've pinned her hair up, like Sadie. She should've touched up her makeup. Ward's accented lilt interrupted the self-reproach. "Dylan knows I'm all about explicit requests." His throat bobbed as he swallowed.

Hazel made a point not to look away. This was one fight she didn't want to back away from. "Was it explicit when you lied to him?"

The music changed once again, a sultry Caribbean rhythm taking over from the heart-pounding techno drums. Two more couples split from the watering hole to join the herd. Hazel merely noticed them out of the corner of her eye. She kept her undivided attention on Ward, the lion camouflaged into a wounded gazelle.

His eyebrows shot up. "When did I lie to him?"

*You're going to make me say it, are you?*

She remembered reading somewhere that sadists were ubiquitous in all walks of life but disproportionately represented among the one percent. Something about power and wealth just drew them out of their shells.

"You told him I checked out," she recalled. "We both know that's not true." It took everything she had not to fist a hand in Ward's silky black shirt and give him a sound shake. She wanted to know why he'd take the trouble to lie for her, but she didn't want to give him the satisfaction of asking outright.

Ward had the nerve to scowl and cock his head, at once bemused and interested. "I haven't the faintest clue what you mean... What did I miss?"

"Bullshit." She wasn't a celebrity, but Hazel Whitley, Dunby native who studied at the University of Missouri for three years before eventually dropping out, couldn't claim anonymity.

"Ah." Ward deliberately set his tumbler on the ice-soaked bar. Already the contents had dipped to half. "You think I should judge you for a youthful mistake."

"Video's still out there. So are the pictures."

"One among many," Ward said, rolling his shoulders as if shaking off the complaint. "We all make errors of judgment. I'm sure you regret it very much." His gaze held hers, gravid with meaning. There was only one right answer to that non-question.

He wanted to see her grovel.

The thought rankled. Hazel rolled her eyes. "Difference being that some of us land on their feet."

Whatever black marks tainted Ward's past, he had the resources to expunge them into obscurity.

"Only because they had a Florence Nightingale to keep them from hitting the floor." He held up his swollen fist and drove home the point with a wince.

Hazel shook her head. No one had asked him to play knight in shining armor. "You really don't know much about throwing a punch, do you?"

"Haven't the foggiest. It's been years since Dylan taught me how to box... And he's a dirty fighter."

"Dylan?" It was hard to imagine. Hazel tried to picture him out of his bespoke worsted wool suits and silk ties, his perfectly coiffed-to-unruliness hair, teaching Ward how to land a punch. It didn't come easy. He didn't have the look of a brawler.

Ward grinned. "Oh yes, hair-pulling and everything. I once saw him kick a boy in the teeth *after* he was down."

"This was at Ledwich?" She struggled to pass it off as an idle question.

Since Dylan had first mentioned the university, Hazel had done her due diligence online. Ward wasn't the only one who could run a Google search. She knew that the school had been founded in the thirties—a rectory transformed into an all-boys academy, then a college. Over the years, it had remained a cloistered but not insignificant stepping stone for a number of well-known moguls and politicians who had gone on to graduate from Harvard and Princeton.

Due to the small size of its facilities and its religious heritage, no women students were admitted, even to this day. Instead, a women's university had been erected two miles away. It had opened its doors in the seventies — a Reaganite solution to a feminist objection.

"Dylan told you about that?" Ward seemed oddly perplexed.

Hazel knew the answer she should give. *He mentioned it in passing, mostly to explain why you and he were you and he.* What came out was a solemn nod.

"Interesting." Ward walked his fingertips around the rim of the whiskey glass, over and over until Hazel started thinking about germs and weird blood and spirits cocktails. Her thoughts had just about run away with her when Ward added, "He despised me back then, you know — with good reason."

"You mean he wasn't desensitized to your winning personality yet?"

The look Ward shot her way was withering. "Most people agree that I have a certain *je ne sais quoi*."

"Most people may need to brush up on their French." Hazel picked up a melting ice cube and pressed it gently to Ward's swelling knuckles. He flinched but didn't retract his hand. "What was he like back then?" *What's he like now? Can I trust him?*

*Will it hurt when he leaves?*

She expected Ward to fire back with a quip of his own, but he was too busy staring at their hands — his bruised and drenched in ice water, hers pale and small by comparison.

"Angry," he said after a beat. "Justifiably so. If you think it's bad being underprivileged, you should try being underprivileged on a remote campus filled with walking, talking trust funds."

"I thought their type usually went to Ivy League schools..." Legacy students were a shoo-in everywhere they went. If not, there always a donation a parent could make, a new library that needed funding. Back in the days when SAT scores meant everything to Hazel, the prospect of a rejection letter had loomed like the sword of Damocles.

She bit her lip when she thought about the shit she'd put her parents through. They were well off by Dunby standards, but there was no way they could have afforded to send their children to upmarket colleges.

Not that it mattered, in the end. Hazel had dropped out in her junior year. She'd never looked back.

"If they can hack it," Ward mused, reeling her back into the present. "If not, Ledwich guarantees networking and a lifetime of job appointments through their alumni network." He met her confusion with a shallow smile. "Dylan grew up in Oakland. He wore plaid and ripped jeans and he'd never even sat in a BMW. He stuck out like a sore thumb... I appreciated that."

"You still do."

Hazel regretted speaking as soon as a shadow fell across Ward's face. In the blink of an eye, he went from fond reminiscence to sullen, closed-off glower. She couldn't backtrack. She had to press on. Here, in a crowded club, with Sadie's inevitable return maybe seconds away, she felt like she was finally about to get some answers.

"You're in love with him, aren't you?"

Ward's features settled into a frosty mask. He removed his hand from beneath hers and shook it out. "My relationship with Dylan is not up for discussion."

"Funny," Hazel shot back, "that's exactly what he said."

But the time for heart-to-hearts was over. Ward had regressed back to cool civility, as if he hadn't just swung a sloppy right hook to defend her honor.

He drew himself up straight as he slid off the bar stool. "It was a pleasure seeing you again, Hazel. Enjoy the rest of your evening."

He disappeared into the crowd before Hazel could stop him. In so doing, he nearly bumped shoulders with a flush-faced Sadie, towing Frank behind her.

They made the perfect couple—giggling, holding hands—and Hazel felt an entirely unjustified pang of envy stab between her ribs. She mustered a smile as they joined her at the bar, but her thoughts were still moored to the slant of Ward's shoulders as he vanished from sight.

# Chapter Eleven

"Are you sure you don't want to stay?"

Hazel nodded for the umpteenth time. "Positive. I'm kind of beat. Think I need to hit the hay." And there was only so much humiliation she could suffer in one night.

Sadie's good intentions notwithstanding, the constant directives to let loose and have a good time were beginning to grate. Hazel had never been particularly adept at shamming joyfulness.

"Okay," Sadie relented, sighing. "But take a cab home. It's late."

"Sure."

They had driven to the club in Frank's battered old Honda Civic—a sensible car for a sensible man. It was still waiting beneath a street lamp when Hazel stepped out of the club and into the frigid night.

Before Frank, Sadie would have wheedled and complained, but she would have left with Hazel when Hazel ran out of steam. Because it was late and because they'd put up with a lot since moving out west, they knew the value of having each other's backs.

*I have my own back, thank you very much.*

Hazel pulled her denim jacket tighter around herself. A salty wind was blowing in from the ocean, stirring tendrils of hair into her eyes. She crossed the street and started toward the bus stop a block and a half away. Splitting cab fare with Sadie was one thing—like splitting the gas bill for the Volvo—but Hazel's insides churned at the thought of covering the expense of a taxi ride out of her fast depleting bank account.

She caught her reflection in a shop window. Her mascara hadn't leaked down her cheeks. Her cat-eye liquid liner had actually held in place. She made a point not to let her gaze dip below the neck, although the black tank top *did* make her breasts seem a little fuller.

She looked *good*, which wasn't a sentiment she was familiar with.

She deserved better than men like Ward deigning to give her the time of day. She certainly deserved better than Dylan, who pretended to be emotionally available but obviously wasn't. *You can't be romantically invested in two people at the same time. It doesn't work.*

Did it? Was she setting feminism back a few decades by refusing to recognize the revolutionary potential of free love? Her thoughts were so engrossing that she didn't notice the tricked-out Mustang crawling by the curb until a voice rang out of the passenger side window.

"You all alone, sweetheart? That's fucking criminal."

Hazel turned. She knew she shouldn't have. Rule number one of life in a big city was keeping your head down, not making eye contact with strangers who accosted you in public places. Rule number two was carrying some sort of defensive weapon — a Taser, for instance, or the pepper spray she'd left on the keychain at home.

The passenger of the Mustang shot the driver a smirk as soon as he saw he had her attention. It wasn't a pleased smile. It was the smile of sharks before they bite your leg off.

"Where're you headed in such a hurry?" asked the man in the passenger seat. He sported sideburns and a baseball cap worn backwards, a loose cotton tee on his otherwise skinny frame.

Hazel's silence did nothing to deter her suitors. They were coming up to a crossroads and the driver was already signaling that he wanted to block her path with the Mustang. He leaned across his buddy to catch Hazel's attention. "Hey, how much for a blow job?"

Anger sparking beneath her veins, Hazel flashed them a glare. "Fuck you."

Tires squealed as the car pulled to an abrupt stop. Hazel saw it happen in slow motion, like something out of a Hollywood movie or a terrible nightmare.

"What did you say, bitch?" Baseball Cap reached for the car door.

Hazel knew what came next. She didn't hang around for confirmation, bolting down the sidewalk as fast as her legs would carry her. Most of the shop windows were dark at this hour, the prospect of business after midnight too unlikely to justify a graveyard shift.

*Where's a Marco's when you need one?*

The first lit storefront she saw might as well have been the pearly gates. Hazel pushed the door open with both hands and spilled inside on wobbly legs.

Breaths wheezed in and out of her chest.

"Uh, we're about to close," said the shopkeeper. Metal rings and studs gleamed on her face like little drops of moonlight.

"I just need a second. There were some guys..." Hazel waved a hand. She had a hard time stringing two words together with her heart jammed in her throat.

Her phone shrilled to life before she could offer a more adequate explanation. Hazel plucked it out with shaking hands. The number that flashed on screen was unfamiliar. She answered anyway.

"So I don't like how we left things," Ward volleyed. "It occurs to me that I was a bit of a jerk—"

"Where are you?"

The question seemed to throw him off his stride. "Uh, on my way to the loft?"

"Can you swing by the club again?" It wasn't far.

"Sure. Do you want to get a drink or..." Ward's accent thickened when he lost control of the conversation. It was something of a relief.

*He's human. Stop the presses.*

"I want you to come get me," Hazel got out, ridiculously pleased when her voice didn't quake. "I'm just down the street, at the..." She glanced around at the corseted mannequins and pink, padded handcuffs. "I'm in the sex shop."

"Interesting choice. I'll be right there."

"Wait." Hazel bit her lip. "Could you stay on the phone with me?"

"Afraid the dildos will attack?" Ward scoffed, but he didn't hang up.

The clerk shot Hazel a puzzled look and held up her own phone — *911* had been keyed onto the screen.

Hazel held her cell away from her face. "Please, I won't be here long. My friend is coming —"

"Did someone hurt you?"

"No... I think they were about to. Maybe." Hazel shrugged. "Police can't help with that." They needed at least a few bruises. A dead body was even better.

A car drove past the shop at that very moment. Hazel flinched back from the door, her stomach sinking. She was dimly aware of Ward saying her name, but her throat was suddenly tight with panic. She focused on breathing. It would be pretty dumb of her to panic when nothing was wrong. *Just us, baby...*

"Sit down," the clerk instructed, wheeling an office chair from behind the till and moving to flip the 'Open/Closed' sign on the door.

Hazel did as instructed.

"You still there?" Ward breathed into the phone. "Hay-zel... I'm five minutes away. Three if I break the speed limit. What's your view on speed limits? Necessary evil or government-sanctioned extortion? If you don't say anything, I'll just keep talking until you get sick of me. Did you ever wonder why we call yellow lights yellow? They're more orange than anything —"

"They're called amber across the pond," Hazel breathed.

"Are they? *Fascinating*. I wonder if it's amber back home, too... Perils of growing up in the wrong country, you see. I don't know anything that truly matters. Nothing about traffic lights, anyway. Ah, there we are — *Venus' Playground*." He sounded like he was reading a sign.

"Guys that bothered you," the clerk said, peering out into the street, "were they driving a BMW?"

Hazel breathed a sigh of relief. "No. That would be my friend." The shiny black car came into view a moment later as Ward double-parked in front of the sex shop. He must have broken a few speed restrictions to get there so fast.

"What was that you were saying earlier about my winning personality?" He shoved the driver side door open wide and stepped out in time for Hazel to make her way out of the shop.

She glanced up and down the street. No sign of the Mustang. It was probably long gone.

Hazel thanked the clerk, who nodded, slid one glance to Ward and his Ritchie Rich blond hair, and went back into the shop. The 'Closed' cardboard sign banged against the door as it fell shut.

"You'll get ticketed," Hazel pointed out. "Double-parking's against the law."

"So is burning red lights, I think, but I don't hear you complaining about that." Ward circled the shiny coupé and opened the passenger door.

Hazel slid in silently. She couldn't think of a quip that wouldn't also imply gratitude.

* * * *

It was hard to say how they wound up at the loft. Maybe it was Ward's doing. He made a few attempts to draw Hazel into conversation, but when she didn't respond he, too, fell silent. Or maybe it was Hazel consciously steering them away from her small, pathetic apartment, protecting the last part of herself that hadn't yet been laid bare for Ward's adjudication.

Whatever the reason, she stepped over the threshold of four-seven-one Aulden Way with a sigh of relief.

"Do you want a drink?" Ward asked, charting a course for the sideboard.

Hazel shook her head. She made her way to the couch and sat, folding her arms over her knees and resting her brow on that makeshift pillow. She was aware of Ward moving about the room—his car keys hitting the artsy glass bowl on the square coffee table, his shiny shoes squeaking as he drew a circuit around the couch. The clinking sounds of a tumbler being filled reached her from very far away.

"Aren't you going to ask what happened?" Hazel asked after a beat. She was used to Sadie grilling her. She was also used to lying to herself and others, because it was the only way to keep anxiety from taking over.

"Figure you'll tell me if you want."

"Reverse psychology," Hazel drawled, "I see." She sat up, spine cracking like logs snapping in a fire. She took the glass Ward pressed into her hands.

"Just soda water and lime."

"You'd tell me if it wasn't?"

Ward rolled his eyes. "And here I thought we were starting to get along..."

"How do you have my phone number?" She'd been foolish enough to put all kinds of information about herself, under her real name, online—never her phone number. In the months and years since she'd dropped out of school, that last shred of anonymity had been her only protection.

Sitting down was a whole operation for Ward. He perched on the edge of the square Barcelona chair, at first, then slid back until the backs of his knees hit the leather upholstery. He folded his long legs, all while balancing a glass of amber liquid in his hands. Probably whiskey, Hazel mused.

"Dylan gave it to me. For emergencies. He's rather paranoid, you may have noticed…"

Hazel had not. "And asking me out counts as an emergency?"

"I wasn't asking you out," Ward scoffed. Where Dylan was all effortless good manners and sophisticated charm, Ward seemed like he was constantly struggling to keep a straight face. Little people either amused or annoyed him. There was no in between.

Right now Hazel was fairly certain that she found herself in the latter category.

"You wanted to talk," she recalled and took a tentative sip of her soda and lime. "What's there to talk about?"

"I'm not sure now is the best time to—"

"You think this hasn't happened before?"

Ward's astonishment flashed starkly across his milky-white features. So Hazel went on.

"It's a rare day when I leave the house without some creep making a pass at me."

"Don't take this the wrong way," Ward replied, "but you *are* a beautiful woman—"

"Right now? Maybe. Not so sure that's true when I'm doing a coffee run in my PJs or wiping spilled ketchup off the tables at Marco's. Or waiting for the bus…."

"Men are pigs?" Ward offered hesitantly.

Hazel took another sip of her soda water. If Ward had slipped her something, then it was subtle enough that she couldn't discern the taste. "Tell me more about you and Dylan in college." She didn't want to talk about herself anymore.

"Wouldn't you rather ask him?"

Hazel toed off her ankle boots. "I'm asking you." *Distract me.*

She expected Ward to refuse. He was as closed off as he'd been at the club, shoulders stiff beneath his tailored black shirt. Yet when he spoke, a wistful smile crept onto his lips, eventually gaining his whole face. He looked different when he smiled in earnest — less Machiavellian, somehow. Certainly less put-together.

"We met in junior year," Ward recalled. "I transferred out of Columbia, failed most of my finals. *Again.* Dylan was on his first go at Ledwich — proud and defiant, huge chip on his shoulder... You have to understand, Ledwich doesn't offer many scholarships. There are anywhere between five and ten students who couldn't otherwise afford tuition, never any more than that. Dylan had been living on campus for three years when I showed up, so most of the abuse from the other students had dwindled by then."

"So you picked up the slack?" Hazel ventured.

She had an easy time imagining Ward as a reckless, arrogant twenty-year-old hell bent on plucking the wings off butterflies just because he could. He wore that mantle even now, albeit not so flagrantly.

He waved a hand. "Every school has its Skull and Crossbones equivalent. Usually it's a fraternity everyone's trying to get into or a football squad that makes grown men wet themselves... We had two rowing teams. Where you fell in the pecking order affected which crew you joined. Scholarship students got the Copperheads." He grimaced. "The rest of us got Even Odds."

"Fitting name," Hazel mumbled under her breath.

"Dylan was desperate to join the Odds. They got the better equipment, the better coach. They had money, essentially, and the Copperheads didn't. He'd been trying to make the crew since freshman year. He showed up for trials every semester... And he was good. Very good. But there was some resistance from the existing members."

"Until you showed up."

Ward narrowed his eyes at the interruption, but he was smiling. "Has Dylan already told you this story?"

"No," said Hazel. "I just have a feeling I know how it goes. You decided to up the stakes, make it harder and harder for him to prove he could make the cut. Dylan dug his heels in. Eventually you came to blows... Ta-da, the start of a wonderful friendship."

The curve of Ward's small smile grew even fainter, smoothing out until his lips were perfectly horizontal. "I told him he'd make the team if he gave me a blow job," he confessed, speaking mostly to his untouched whiskey.

Hazel arched her eyebrows. "He turned you down? Punched you in the face?"

"No."

It wasn't the feel-good homoerotic coming of age movie she'd built up in her head. It also wasn't something Ward seemed to treat as hilariously funny. His shoulders stooped when he shifted forward to set his tumbler on the coffee table. He didn't seem proud or commanding anymore.

He didn't seem like he wanted to relive the past.

*So this is what guilt looks like when it's packaged in Hugo Boss.* Her stomach roiled as she ran through scathing remarks in her head, discarding them one right after the other. In the end, she only wanted to know one more thing. "Why?"

Ward glanced up from his joined palms with a sullen expression. His prayers to the god of hard liquor and bad decisions must have gone unheeded.

"I wanted him. He didn't want me... I never said it was a cheerful story."

Something about his posture told Hazel that he was perfectly aware the addendum did nothing to exculpate him. She didn't heed it.

"And now?"

"Now?"

Hazel couldn't tell if he was stalling her or not, but she furrowed her brow all the same. "What do you want from him now? You haven't told him about my — indiscretions. You wanted to set the record straight tonight..." If this was Ward's way of working his way toward absolution, Hazel wanted no part in it. "Dylan mentioned that he's been with other women since you and he left school," she pointed out, disregarding the part where he was also adamant that his relationship with Ward was off limits.

He'd made clear that a relationship with him would imply putting up with his tetchy roommate. There was no way around it. Before she'd found out that Ward was an abusive fuck, Hazel might have considered it. Now, her skin crawled. She'd been the Dylan in that equation. She knew it was messed up.

"I want him to be happy," Ward confessed miserably.

"Even if that means being with other people?"

Ward held out for a long beat before nodding, once and solemnly, and glancing away.

"Is it because they're women or..." Hazel pursed her lips. "Is it a fetish thing?" Dylan had a fully fitted playroom. Clearly his taste for dominating women wasn't a passing fetish.

"Partly. Dylan will submit to me if I ask. But since I don't reciprocate, I can't help feeling like I'm forcing him into something he doesn't truly care for."

*Like the first time, you mean?* Hazel scoffed, which had the same effect as that jagged barb.

Ward flinched. He had no right to look so downtrodden, so hurt. He'd gotten everything he wanted out of that stupid dare all those years back — and Dylan was still around, still caught in his orbit. Some men were lucky like that.

"He wouldn't be sleeping with you in the first place if he didn't enjoy it on some level."

She didn't want to admit it, but sex with Dylan was at once intimate and personal. Even at their most clinical, their sessions in his playroom had never felt like they could involve any other two people. Dylan made her the center of his world in exchange for her trust. Whether or not that was a fair trade, Hazel couldn't say. She trusted herself less than she did him.

Body language at odds with his tone, Ward asked, "What makes you think we're sleeping together?"

Hazel narrowed her eyes. *Really?*

Ward scowled but ducked his head. "It's complicated."

"That's what he said." Like most things, the snappy comeback was funnier in her head.

"You must think I'm a terrible person."

"You're not stellar. That's for sure." The retort seemed to diminish Ward even further, as if her words were millstones piled onto his shoulders. Were she in a more vindictive mood, Hazel could see herself deriving great pleasure from giving Ward the verbal lashing he deserved. It didn't seem necessary. He wasn't sitting there, hunch shouldered, and telling her all this because he was *proud*.

On impulse, Hazel exchanged her glass for his and downed the whiskey in one burning swig. "I'll need to be a lot drunker before I start confessing my sins," she offered by way of explanation. Then she held out the glass. "Another."

Surprise flitting off his features, Ward complied.

# Chapter Twelve

"Your bag's moving."

"What?" Hazel tried to sit up, but she was lying on her hair and the unexpected tug stabbed through her skull. "Ow!"

Ward laughed. He'd been laughing a lot, when he wasn't angrily swiping at his eyes. "Your bag," he repeated. He hooked a toe in the offending accessory and nudged it against her calves.

It was, indeed, vibrating.

Hazel plucked out her cell. "Oh... It's my sister-in-law."

"Answer," Ward urged. "You can tell her about the dent you've put in my stash of Glenfiddich." He swirled his tumbler in her direction as though to underscore the point. Somewhere around the third refill, he'd brought the bottle along to the sitting area. He reached for it now, pulling off the metal cap with his teeth.

Even sloppy drunk, he should've been easy to ignore.

"It's a Facebook update," Hazel shot back. She negotiated the complicated mechanics of couch and unbound hair carefully, folding her bare feet under her lotus-style. "Ooh, college reunion! I guess she forgot I didn't graduate..."

"Maybe that's why she invited you."

Hazel fished one of her boots off the floor and lobbed it in Ward's general direction. As projectiles went, it didn't have much spin. Her aim left a lot to be desired. The boot flew past the Eames chair and landed with a dull thump on the hardwood floor.

"Shut up. I like Rhonda."

"Cool name," Ward gushed, unruffled. The way he held up his hand made Hazel think of an airplane. One that crashed on his knee, fingers warped into a fist. "Very middle America."

For want of better ammo, Hazel brandished the phone at him in a loose circle. "You calling my sister *average*?"

"Please. There's nothing wrong with average! Average is pancakes and string cheese, and those little crackers shaped like animals," he said and ended with a hiccup.

"Like *Ward* is any better..."

"I'll have you know it's my father's name," he slurred. "Which I suppose only proves the point."

Hazel didn't try very hard to conceal a smirk. "And here I thought *I* had a tough relationship with my folks."

"How many siblings have you got?"

She held up two fingers, the back of her hand turned toward him.

Ward smirked. "See, that's what I mean." He tapped his thumb against his chest. "Only child."

"*Millionaire* only child." The distinction was worth making.

He brushed her off. "The millions are tied up in more lawsuits than I can count... Most of which we'll probably lose." His tumbler was the target of a particularly dark glare before Ward tipped it against his lips. He downed the last of his whiskey with a single bob of the throat. "Sometimes I reckon Dylan's right. I *should* cut and run. Start over... I could open a rival fast food chain, give you a run for your money." His smile was ugly and mean, but Hazel had a hard time mustering the appropriate dread.

"You know Dylan a lot better than I do... Is he usually right?"

"Usually." Ward held her gaze. "But he's also idealistic. Suppose it comes from being adopted by hippies. Did you know his mother runs a community center? If you ever have a burning desire to take up hip-hop with a gaggle of octogenarians, ask Dylan to put you in touch."

Hazel scoffed, dismissing the suggestion out of hand. "Yeah, because I'm sure Dylan'll want to introduce me to his folks." She tried not to wonder why it was so easy to say as much to Ward, whom she didn't even like, when Dylan still left her tongue-tied. Was there no middle ground between eggshells and hot coals?

"Why not?"

"How many submissives has he paraded around to friends and family?"

She could see the calculation in Ward's eyes before he shook his head. "You're selling him short," he protested, sounding fractionally more sober than before. "He's a good guy." The bottle of Glenfiddich was tipped against the lip of the tumbler, amber liquor once again harnessing the diffuse mood lighting in the loft and reflecting it back onto Ward's fingers like leopard spots.

"You don't have to convince me."

Ward's scowl deepened the dimples on either side of his mouth. "What's this, then? Fishing for compliments?"

"From you? God help me!" Hazel shook her head. "I'm just making conversation... Least I can do, after you nearly broke your hand trying to defend my honor."

He looked down at his bruised knuckles, gritting his teeth when the purpling thumb shook instead of flexing obediently. "Lucky I was there, huh?"

"Lucky the *other* guy was alone."

The spat could've led to a very different outcome if Ward had had to take on Lothario *and* Lothario's buddies. He conceded the point with a rueful grin, two spots of color blooming high on the apples of his cheeks. "You don't think I could've taken him on with my kung-fu? I'm pretty badass when provoked. It's like poking one of them grizzlies."

"You," Hazel said pointedly, "are a drunk."

Ward burst out laughing, whiskey splashing onto his black slacks. "*A* drunk? Fine, then *you're* a liar."

It might have been the booze, but disbelief curdled in her belly.

"How am I a liar?"

"You hate Rhonda." Ward fanned his fingers and twirled his hand around as though to encapsulate her person. "It's written on your face. Is it 'cause she's all smarty pants?"

"She's a housewife," Hazel snapped. Her face fell as soon as the words were past her lips. "Fuck, I didn't mean that."

Ward's grin made it hard to retract the careless charge.

"I didn't mean it. She's going to be a mom. She made her choice…"

"And you don't think much of it. That's okay. Would have to turn in your feminist card if you didn't have *strong opinions* about motherhood."

Glare aside, Hazel couldn't totally dismiss the kernel of truth. She stared her cell down, the invite still flashing merry in blue and white. "Truth is I'd probably be doing the same thing in her shoes."

"Waiting tables isn't your dream job, huh?"

*We can't all be CEOs.* Hazel scowled. "Thanks for rubbing it in, asshole." Liquor made it easier to run her mouth.

"Hey, running a virtually bankrupt company isn't all it's cracked up to be, either, you know…"

"Talk to me when your tits are splattered all over the Internet," Hazel shot back, seeing red. She snatched the whiskey bottle out of Ward's hands and replenished her glass. "I can't go to an interview without wondering if the guy sitting across the table spent last night jerking off to my naked ass."

Ward arched his eyebrows, something unsympathetic and curious in his gaze. "And the lesson here is that next time you should think more carefully before making a sex tape."

*There will never be a next time.* Not that the first had been her doing, either.

Hazel doused the memory in single malt. She could barely taste the oak casks anymore.

"How come you dropped out?" Ward asked, seemingly out of the blue. Hazel doubted the thought had only just come to him. She was beginning to understand how his mind worked. Even hammered, he wasn't stupid. He'd saved up the question, waiting until she'd finished railing against the world to back her into a corner.

"I packed up all my shit and left campus. That's how."

"Yes, but… Why?" Ward inclined his head against the backrest of the lounge chair. "Was it because of the sex tape?"

*Completely.*

When Hazel didn't dismiss the suggestion out of hand, he frowned. "I know you Americans are fiendishly puritanical about these things, but it's not like coeds don't get up to worse. All those campus parties…"

"It's not so simple. I had a scholarship." *A reputation. A family.*

*A boyfriend.*

"With a morality clause?" Ward shifted his weight, elbows balanced on his knees. Was this what he was like in board meetings? Liquor buzzing in her veins, Hazel tried to picture him focusing those dark eyes on dull financial reports. Yet the mental image that rose behind her closed lids was that of Ward peering at Dylan when he thought his friend wasn't looking. She could well believe he was capable of taking what he wanted, but there was a weird sort of tenderness to him, as well.

Hazel made a mental note to watch her step. Hidden depths abounded here.

She licked her lips. "There was a GPA requirement. I had to keep a B plus average." She rolled her shoulders, trying to play it off. This was all ancient history, rendered meaningless by the passage of time and the choices she'd made since. "I didn't perform."

"I thought you said it was because of the tape."

"*You* said that," she corrected, never happier for holding her tongue than she was then.

Ward held her gaze. "You didn't protest... And you protest *everything* I say."

"I'm drunk. Cut me some slack, Columbo." It would've been a passable excuse, were it not for the whiskey sharpening instead of dulling the bite of memory. She downed the dregs and reached for the bottle again. Ward was faster.

He caught her hand, fingers feverish around her wrist. His gaze zipped across her features as though he was searching for the Rosetta Stone that would help him decipher the inner workings of her brain. "What am I missing here?"

"Oh, honey," Hazel drawled, laughing mirthlessly. "How long have you got?"

Ward let her have the bottle.

* * * *

Tracts on the noticeboards of college campuses across the country laid out very good reasons for not drinking with strange men. Hazel wondered if any of those lists featured 'waking up in bed with your maybe-boyfriend's significant other'.

If so, those rape-prevention tacticians really thought of everything.

If not, it was something they should look into. Because it was fucking awkward.

The bedroom resolved around her in fragments— first a sliver of the floor-to-ceiling windows reluctantly letting light in through their many panes and splashing it across the unvarnished hardwood floors, then the mahogany dresser. The self-standing mirror in the corner caught her eye when she rolled over. It reflected a slice of the bed beneath the sleeve of a discarded black shirt.

The whole room belonged in a fancy hotel, but Hazel instinctively knew that wasn't the case.

She scrubbed a hand over her face, envisioning the smudged makeup, the tangle of blonde hair doubtlessly shedding all over Ward's pristine pillowcases. Her mouth was dry from too much whiskey and not enough water, but she didn't feel sick. Her head was blissfully, traitorously free of migraines, and she needed to use the facilities.

She spent a moment contemplating a swift escape — possibly by way of fleeing naked into the street and getting herself arrested for indecent exposure — but there was no point. The other side of the mattress dipped as Ward turned onto his back. Between the crisscrossing lines the pillow had dented into his cheek and the flattened hair just above his right temple, his expression was open and tranquil. His lashes fluttered.

"Hey," Hazel croaked out. *Remember me? Crazy woman you got drunk last night. How's it going?*

Ward smiled. "Hey." That decidedly un-Ward-like lightness was short-lived. He pushed himself upright, covers rolling down his body as he propped himself against the pillows. "Shit, did we—?"

"I don't think so." Hazel peeled back the sheets and looked down at her body. She was still wearing her underwear and tank top. And Ward seemed to have pulled on pajama bottoms before they had crashed. Into the *same* bed.

Together.

"That whiskey's killer," Hazel mumbled as she swung her legs over the edge of the mattress and gave

Ward her back. She rubbed the grit from her eyes, but that didn't help reality improve.

Behind her, Ward made a sound halfway between a chuckle and a sigh. He didn't disagree. His silence stretched past the bounds of the question and into the murky gray of shared discomfort.

"Are you okay?" he asked at length.

"Did you fall and hit your head?"

"No, I'm just—"

Hazel couldn't bear to let him finish. Non-asshole Ward was only palatable when she was chugging back big-ticket Scotch. "Worried I'll press charges?"

The joke fell flat in light of last night's heart-to-heart. She winced.

"Sorry. I didn't mean that… I'm fine, just—not much of a morning person." She finger-combed her hair back, trying for some semblance of dignity. What was she thinking, getting into bed with Ward?

More importantly, what was *he* doing letting her?

She startled when she felt the bedsprings dip. The touch of a hand on her upper arm froze her in place. Ward knee-walked his way closer to brush her hair from her shoulder. Then he pressed his lips to the patch of skin just south of her tank strap.

"There," he rasped. "Now you have something to press charges for."

Hazel wanted to snort with laughter. *Of course, you would think of that.* But the attempt died in her throat. When Ward didn't retreat, she turned fractionally and met his ink-black eyes. "How much do you remember about last night?"

She could see Ward weighing his answer, considering the face-saving benefits of a lie for both of them. "Everything," he said.

"Me too."

"Good whiskey'll do that…"

He'd dropped his voice an octave, not unlike an invitation. Hazel unconsciously found herself leaning in — to hear him better, obviously — and stayed for the caress of his breaths on her lips. She didn't wait for him to draw another before obliterating the gap between them.

A tiny voice at the back of her mind whispered that she was moving too fast in the wrong direction, that jeopardizing everything she could have with Dylan was a terrible move. She paid it no heed. Strategy games had never held her attention for long and Ward was warm and sturdy and *present*. Last night's well-oiled chat had rattled her cage so badly.

She needed an anchor. She needed to figure out where she stood. *I'm so sorry, Dylan…*

Her unspoken apology fell by the wayside as Ward cupped her cheek and brushed the tip of his tongue to her lips. It was a no-brainer. Hazel granted him passage, shifting forward to press herself into his arms in greedy offering.

Ward growled low in his throat, a menacing, heady sound that traveled straight to her cunt. Hazel had a brief moment of clear-headed doubt — *This is wrong, we shouldn't be doing this* — before Ward stole her breath completely. His biceps clenched beneath her timid touch. At first she thought it was some kind of hair-trigger. She started to ask, but Ward made short work of the attempt as he flipped her under him.

The kisses grew steadier, less tentative.

When he palmed her breast, Hazel rocked her pelvis up to get friction where she needed it most. Ward moved like Dylan in so many ways — taking his time tasting her lips before he dipped his head to the curve of her neck, touching — memorizing the uncharted planes of her body without grabbing—that she wondered what he'd be like if they were to retire to Dylan's playroom.

She aborted that line of thought. No matter how sexy, how twisted, it wouldn't be right.

Hazel ground out a moan when she felt Ward scrape his teeth deliciously against her jugular. She tangled one hand in his shirt and the other in his hair, holding him in place.

Ward surged into the kiss when she tightened her fingers, dropping his hips to hers. Sensation shorted out Hazel's breaths. Ward was half hard already, erection tenting the flimsy fabric of his sleep pants.

A flood of liquid heat settled low in Hazel's belly as their caresses grew increasingly frantic. She had to bring one arm down so that Ward could slide the strap of her tank top from her shoulder, which seemed as good a reason as any to drag her fingertips down the arch of his spine and dig her fingernails in when he bent his mouth to her breast.

The way he swirled his tongue around her nipple was *all* Dylan. The thought should have made Hazel feel ashamed, but all she could think of was how good it felt. She wondered belatedly if Dylan and Ward had slept with the same woman before. It didn't seem to matter that much once Ward started sucking in earnest.

Hazel curled her toes into the bedding, hips arching helplessly. He wasn't gentle about it. The soft, snug circle of his lips contrasted with the rough swipe of his tongue and the sharp pressure of teeth, much in the same way that Dylan's leather crop had elicited small, pained noises that quickly gave way to rapturous delight.

Ward liberated her of her tank top and bra in short order, then sat back on his haunches—a wild look in his eyes—and skimmed his fingertips to her panties. Something in his expression told Hazel that this was her last chance to get off the rollercoaster ride. She arched her back, twisting to make it easier on him to remove her underwear. Take-backs were not an option.

He wasted no time throwing the scrap of silk over the edge of the bed and palming her sex with a rough—almost proprietary—hand. He wasn't gentle about it.

Hazel threw her head back. "Fuck, yes…"

Dylan had put his mouth on her after trussing her up in his playroom. She expected something similar from Ward.

It wasn't to be.

He took her knees in his hands and slid his broad palms to her ankles, where he seized a rough hold. Air turned to soup in her lungs as he nudged her none too gently onto her belly.

A shiver of anticipation, half dread and half desire, skittered down Hazel's spine, but she moved with him. She didn't think to offer resistance.

Submission was deeply ingrained, part of the way she'd always been with her partners. She couldn't make up the difference now.

The bedside drawer jerked open, then slammed shut. Foil crinkled. Hazel pushed herself up onto her elbows and twisted around at the waist.

Ward caught her eye as he slid a condom down his stiff cock. He was thicker than she'd expected and he tended slightly to the left. Unlike Dylan, he was also uncircumcised. *My first,* Hazel thought deliriously, and obediently turned her head when Ward sank a hand into her hair and pulled—and pulled.

He had her arch her spine as far as she could stand before lightly caressing her sex with his length. The latex slid wetly against her folds, spikes of pleasure stabbing at her clit when he zeroed in on that tiny, engorged nub of flesh.

Dylan might have asked if she was sure before thrusting inside. Ward did not. He held her still as he aligned them, then rocked his hips forward. There was nowhere for Hazel to go—not that she would've wanted to—and the illusion of being immobilized cranked her engine in an all-too-primitive sort of way.

It was the leather swing all over again, only this time she wasn't afraid of bringing down the shoddy metal rigging. She wasn't worried about making a fool of herself. A moan tore from her throat as he slid in deep, one smooth movement joining them almost to the hilt.

Ward reached for her right arm without warning. Also without warning, he tugged on her wrist until Hazel had no choice but to remove it from the mattress. She panted, torn between the sharp sting in her scalp and the low, delicious burn in her nether regions—and now the distant fear of falling face first into the bed sheets. Ward withdrew slowly, only to press back in, hard and deep, curling her toes with a flash of delight. His grunts and hissing breaths speared the silence of the bedroom.

Sweat gathered in Hazel's collarbones and dripped from her upper lip to her tongue. She barely tasted the salt as euphoria coiled around her, slow at first, then faster and faster, a supernova building in the pit of her stomach. Ward fucked her at a merciless pace. She didn't think she could come without at least a little clitoral stimulation—it hadn't happened before, anyway—but Ward didn't give her much wiggle room. The vise-tight grip he held on her forearm coupled with the rapid-fire snap of his hips and the staccato burst of their ragged breaths marched her right up to the edge.

Pleasure soared, that familiar sense of coming untethered from her own body seeping into her bloodstream like a drug.

She was dimly aware of nonsensical pleas spilling from her tongue, but she had little thought for what, exactly, she was saying. Orgasm struck gradually, crumbling her defenses bit by bit. Every muscle in her body locked tight. Her left arm gave out as Ward released his grip on her hair, but she wasn't allowed to sink down to the bed.

Ward grasped her hips with both hands, slamming into her with jagged grunts. Aftershocks ignited beneath Hazel's skin, sensation running the gamut from too much to not enough, then back again. Tighter and tighter, Ward angling just right to brush against her G-spot, until Hazel didn't know if what she was feeling was just the aftermath of her first orgasm or another burst of bliss bubbling in her veins. She made a noise halfway between a plea and a mangled iteration of Ward's name, distantly aware of his rhythm falling apart as he chased his own high.

It was that as much as anything else that fanned the smoldering coals of her arousal.

There was nothing of Dylan in the way Ward let himself crumble, his breaths hot on Hazel's shoulder blade. He rocked into her with sharp, sloppy jerks, even as he came down from his high, holding her captive where she lay.

Hazel turned her head against the tangled bed sheets and blew out the strands of snarled hair in her eyes. She couldn't see much of Ward, just the top of his head, dirty-blond hair sticky with perspiration and the curve of his right eyebrow, cocked as if in surprise. His other eyebrow seemed out of commission.

"So," she breathed, "are we going to blame the whiskey for this, too?"

She almost feared that Ward hadn't heard her. Then his body shook against hers, a guffaw creeping out from deep in his belly. "Bit late for that, don't you think?"

Hazel thought so, but then again, she wasn't really talking about the whiskey. *I just fucked my maybe-boyfriend's significant other.* What would the campus flyers have to say about that?

# Chapter Thirteen

While Ward endeavored to get breakfast going, Hazel retreated to the shower. She was unconvinced that Dylan and Ward stocked anything edible in their minimalist kitchen, but the morning had been rich in surprises already. She welcomed a moment of respite. Orgasm had left her slick and sluggish, her knees creaking as she shivered under the warm spray.

*Okay. That really happened.*

The vain, gleeful thought of calling Sadie flashed through her mind. It was usually the other way around—Sadie indulging in ill-fated one-night stands while Hazel held the moral high ground—and she didn't think it likely that something like this would happen again.

She used Ward's shampoo and body wash, bathing herself in his woodsy scent like the traitor she was. The bathroom was all black tile and gleaming mirrors. Six spotlights cast their warm glow over the shiny floor, neither blinding nor making the room seem drab and cavernous. Everything about the loft was perfectly calibrated for luxury. Even the joints between the sleek marble slabs had been buffed to a shine—no doubt by some specialized cleaning company.

Not for the first time, Hazel recognized that she was completely out of her depth.

She set aside the thought as she wrapped herself in a fluffy gray towel and wrung out her hair. She had every intention of getting dressed as soon as she returned to the bedroom, but the sound of Ward's voice downstairs stopped her short.

Red flags sprouted like mushrooms after rain.

She lingered at the top of the stairs for a long moment, flexing her toes into the wooden boards. There was no second voice, no sign that Ward had welcomed some other visitor into the loft while she was showering.

"You wouldn't believe who I ran into last night," he boasted.

Hazel's heart performed a complicated Cirque du Soleil-worthy somersault. "Let's call her your favorite kind of nut… What? Isn't that enough of a hint?"

Hazel perked up her ears, but no matter how she strained, she couldn't discern the voice on the other end of the line. The penny only dropped when Ward named the speaker.

"I stand corrected. Oh, relax. She's actually not that bad, Dylan. We're getting along like a house on fire."

*Dylan?* Hazel steadied herself with a hand on the banister. She wanted to sit down before her knees buckled. She wanted to go downstairs and snatch the phone out of Ward's hands. Why hadn't Dylan called her? What was he waiting for?

Ward laughed, a strange and unfettered sound, more heartfelt than his habitual snigger. "All right, man, I'll let you get some sleep… If you have to ask, then you don't know me at all." He ended on a scoff, his cell sliding to the kitchen counter with a telltale click.

Hazel padded the rest of the way downstairs. "How is he?"

"Jesus!" Ward jumped back from the French press, one hand pressed to his ribcage as though to keep his heart from leaping out. "You scared the shit out of me."

*You'll live.* "Ward."

"He's fine! Peachy fucking keen." The Ward who had lain in bed and laughed with her less than an hour ago was nowhere to be seen. This was his familiar twin, Mr. Hyde. "He's flying back Friday."

"Isn't that early? I thought he was staying until the end of the weekend —"

Ward waved a hand. "Change of plans, I suppose. No doubt he'll give you all the details as soon as he lands."

Unfazed by Ward's snippy tone, Hazel slotted onto a padded leather stool by the breakfast area of the kitchen island. The steel footrest was cold beneath her bare toes. She curled one foot into the other, holding up the towel with her arms tucked close around her body. This was one conversation that couldn't wait for clothes.

"Did you tell him?"

To his credit, Ward didn't feign ignorance. "A trans-Pacific phone call doesn't really seem like the best venue to inform my best friend that I've fucked his girlfriend, does it?" He slid a dainty, square cup before her and filled it with steaming black coffee from the French press. "Like I said, he'll be back Friday. You can tell him all about how I plied you with liquor then."

Hazel nearly spat her coffee all over the granite countertop. "How you did what?" She wiped her lips with the back of a hand. "Is this delayed-effect hangover?"

Ward's scowl broadened, features dark behind the rim of his cup, but he didn't reply.

"So that's what you want to go with? Coercion?" The pit fell out of her stomach. Ward's white knighting notwithstanding, his sudden martyrdom threw her for a loop. "You and I must remember last night very differently. I seem to recall *asking* for a glass of whiskey." *And for the five that followed.*

Stubborn, Ward stuck to his guns—namely silence and sneer.

They left Hazel in an unprecedented predicament. "You're kidding me, right?" *I slept with you because I wanted to, asshole. You think I can't tell the difference between being badgered and being accommodated?*

"You should leave," Ward said, speaking to his mug more so than to Hazel.

"You're throwing me out? That's a low blow... Even for you." All the snappy comebacks in the world couldn't take away the sting of his glare or the arch dismissal in those three little words.

Ward wanted her gone.

Speaking to Dylan must've done a number on him. Hazel's ego was too bruised for her to give a damn. She pushed away from the kitchen island, leaving behind delicious coffee and stuck-up, spineless one-night stand. Her bare feet and long towel prevented a dramatic exit—all the more reason to let aggravation simmer in her bloodstream. Hazel donned last night's clothes in haste.

"Do you need a—?"

"No," she snapped, tugging on her ankle boots. "I don't need anything from you." Her wet hair spilled across her shoulder as she straightened, momentarily obscuring Ward from view. She spun around with one hand on the loft door, meeting his glower with one of her own. "Call me when you grow a pair."

As she wrenched open the door, Hazel caught one last glimpse of Ward. He was calmly drinking his morning coffee, a now-familiar scowl twisting at his features.

\* \* \* \*

Time seemed to slow dramatically over the course of the following week. Hazel embraced the routine of home, diner, home, rebuffing Sadie's attempts to coax her to a club again. Her last attempt had left a pleasant ache between her legs and a not so pleasant throbbing in her chest.

She didn't call Ward.

The urge came and went, mostly when she was stuck at a red light or tossing and turning in bed. And just as she didn't call him, Dylan didn't deign to call her.

Solitude had never been particularly enjoyable, but it was worse after a brief glimpse of the alternative. There were nights when Hazel woke up thinking she was back at the loft, one insignificant part of Dylan's strange, unorthodox relationship with Ward. Then she'd open her eyes and glimpse the lump of the laundry hamper in the corner of the bedroom or the twisted aluminum blinds — or the apartment across the street, with its shriveled azaleas in cracked window boxes. Flashes of her drab, lonely bedroom plucked her from the arms of Morpheus. They made for a rude awakening.

Hazel tried to disguise the festering hurt. She thought she had it under control, until one afternoon after her shift when she spotted Ward's BMW across the street, idling in the muggy heat.

He lowered the passenger side window. "Give you a ride home?"

"I have a car, thanks." *What are you doing here?* The question rose to the tip of her tongue, then ebbed back. She reminded herself that she didn't care. "Anything else?"

It was too much to hope that he regretted their last chat.

Ward tapped ash into the slot in the center console. The lit end of his cigarette burned amber as he sucked smoke into his lungs. "Can we talk?"

Hazel weighed her options. *Yes* would be another zigzag between landmines and buried skeletons, another reminder that Ward was testing her patience the better to report to Dylan when he got back.

"What do you want?" she asked instead. Straight answers were overrated anyway.

The short-lived hint of a wrinkle between Ward's eyebrows told her all she needed to know. He hadn't come to apologize. He didn't feel bad about throwing her out on account of buyer's remorse. Hazel squeezed the car door with both hands and pushed off.

"Go home, Ward. I'm too tired for this shit."

"Dylan wanted me to check on you," he called out, too brusque to be anything but truthful.

Hazel froze in her steps. They'd spoken again. Why did that hurt? Why did she feel neglected? Dylan had made clear that he was giving her time to figure out where they stood. He hadn't claimed that the same terms applied to Ward.

*We're not the same.* Ward had power over Dylan. Now he was looking to sink his claws into Hazel, too.

"Tell Dylan I do just fine without a babysitter," she shot over her shoulder.

"What happened to being accosted by creeps every miserable day?"

Hazel whirled around so fast that her handbag slapped her thigh. "I must be moving up in the world 'cause they don't usually drive BMWs." The windshield was awash with the red and purple hues of the setting sun, a ribbon of airplane exhaust dividing Ward's face into warmth and chill down the length of his nose. "Anything else, creep?"

Ward put up the passenger side window. The engine revved at the turn of the key. Hazel watched him pull away with an abrupt turn. She didn't think Ward even checked his mirrors. Playing fast and loose with six-figure cars was just another benefit of wealth—one more reminder that she and Ward had nothing in common besides Dylan—and even there, they were better off keeping their distance.

Hazel peeled a stray curl from her lips, grimacing at the sticky texture of smeared lip gloss. It wasn't her fault that Dylan didn't have better friends.

*It's not Ward's fault that you can't be civil*, a small voice taunted. The lapse of judgment weighed on Hazel's shoulders as much as Ward's. She couldn't brush it off or pretend they hadn't crossed a line.

She locked down the thought before it could spiral out of control. Ward would have to try harder if he was hoping to get under her skin.

She wasn't about to be run off.

* * * *

After her last foray into the clubbing scene, Hazel's inclination had dwindled to nearly nothing. But there were only so many nights she could spend catching up with *Real Housewives*, or commiserating with wannabe supermodel flunkees before her eyes began to glaze over. When that happened, the self-sabotaging quadrants in her brain faithfully sent her back, retracing steps and digging up old hurt to sample again.

Time to kill always made for easy self-flagellation. Hazel took about as much of that as she could. It wasn't until she started flirting with the thought of poking her sister-in-law on Facebook that she understood how deep and how fast she was sinking.

*This is why I don't date.* Bitter shame kindled in her gut as she pushed up from the couch and switched off the TV. A cursory glance of the living room unearthed her cell.

Hazel was halfway through scrolling to Sadie's contact when she remembered — Sadie was with Frank tonight. She'd borrowed the car for that purpose, too, with the promise of filling up the tank before she picked Hazel up in the morning.

"Crap," she muttered to the silent apartment.

The wrench in the works didn't stop her from grabbing her boots and tugging them on forcefully. There were always buses. Cabs. She tamped down the flicker of anxiety that threatened to invade her bloodstream and latched the door in her wake.

She had little memory of the ride to the club. The heat of the day still clung close to the ground, forced down by leaden cloud. Hazel's tank top stuck to her shoulder blades, an unpleasant, damp compress instantly chilled by the AC that gusted inside Sadie's favorite watering hole.

Hazel squeezed her way through the swarm of bodies, charting a straight-shot route to the bar. She'd picked this place because she knew it, because familiarity counted. The top-shelf whiskey was just a nice addition. Hazel wasted no time in ordering herself a Wild Turkey double with enough ice that the condensation on the glass made her palm slippery-wet. Peace and quiet were out of the question in the club. Some Lady Gaga remix stuttered out of the concealed speakers, filling her ears with mangled innuendo. Her ribcage rattled with the bass line. Her demons couldn't compete.

"You're going to think I'm stalking you," a familiar voice said over her shoulder.

Her demons might have been hard-pressed to lay into her, but Ward was flesh and blood, and difficult to ignore on a good day.

Hazel squared her shoulders but didn't turn. "Depends... Did Dylan ask you to do that, too?" If she didn't face him, she could pretend she wasn't lobbing hurt at an easy target.

"I thought you'd sworn off hard liquor," Ward replied, sidestepping the question. He was quick to take advantage of the freshly vacated bar stool next to Hazel's and seemingly all too eager to take her silence for an invitation.

"Don't worry," said Hazel, "I'm not counting on letting anyone bully me into bed tonight. Got a strict once-a-week policy."

"Right."

The lights in the club might have been low and the music loud, but Ward was easy to read in spite of the dizzying cacophony.

"Clutch that beer any tighter and you'll be pulling glass shards out of your hand," Hazel mused. His knuckles were white around the neck of the bottle. She wondered if he was daydreaming of squeezing her neck instead.

"Let's not pretend you give a damn about the state of my hands."

"Yeah," Hazel agreed, "that's why we sat here the first time... 'Cause I don't give a damn." She couldn't resist meeting his eyes for long. Part of her was curious if he could hold her gaze and hang onto his glorified moaning. The rest wondered at the damage she'd made.

Ward thinned his lips and looked away. "He still doesn't know."

*Of course, it all comes back to Dylan.*

"Why?"

"Didn't know how to tell him," Ward confessed, raising the bottle to take a swig. "Least I can do is wait until he's close enough to kick me in the teeth."

"Oh, he strikes me as the kind to book an earlier flight if he feels compelled to settle a score." Hurt prompted the jibe rather than experience. Dylan had been nothing but patient with her. It was Ward who constantly rammed her foundations. "Was I that bad?" Hazel wondered aloud. She shrugged in the face of his scowl. "You're in such a hurry to write me off that I figure it must've been a sub-par experience."

It hadn't been. His tooth-grinding moans still echoed between her ears. His tight hold lived on in the bruises he'd left on her hips.

Ward scraped his thumbnail over the tinted bottle, peeling up the label. "Wasn't bad."

"Easy, tiger. Compliments like that... You'll make me blush."

"It can't happen again," Ward muttered, unflinchingly morose despite her needling. "You get that, right? It was a mistake."

"No shit." Dylan was one of the good ones, but even good guys had a habit of expecting fidelity. No matter how open-minded, chances were he wouldn't be good with what she'd done.

Hazel downed her whiskey in a less than ladylike fashion. *So much for clearing my head.*

"Thing is, I have no intention of letting you take the heat alone," she told Ward. He wasn't the one who had made the first move. That blame rested with Hazel.

She nudged him with her elbow. "I know you've got this whole theory about liquor and...what we did." No doubt that was where Dylan had picked it up. "But it wasn't like that. Believe me, I know the difference between tipsy and three sheets to the wind."

"Your ex?" Ward asked. He seemed more guarded than convinced.

"Yeah."

"Is... Is that who we have to thank for the home movie?"

It was Hazel's turn to avoid his gaze. The last thing she wanted was to further spoil her evening by dredging up that mess.

But Ward was dogged. He dug his heels in. "What happened there?"

Hazel shook her head, hunting for an appropriate deflection—an answer that would sound convincing without giving him much to go on. Nothing came to mind. Against her will, memories unspooled behind her eyes, every flicker of the strobe lights a camera flash. "Think I'm gonna head home," she said in the end, groping into her handbag for her wallet.

"Something I said?"

In the shaky, dizzying lights, Ward's features were painted a stark, cadaverous white. He looked both more and less than human.

"Yeah," Hazel admitted, too quiet to be heard but too obvious for Ward to misunderstand.

"You okay to drive?"

"Don't have the car. I'll catch a taxi—"

"I'll give you a ride," Ward said, slapping down a few crisp bills and planting his beer on top to hold them in place. "Come on," he entreated when Hazel dithered. "Thought you liked the BMW."

She did. It was a cool car and the leather upholstery was like butter to the touch. But Ward's favors were honey-traps, delivered with an invisible price tag. She considered turning him down. The words rose to the tip of her tongue, a stubborn lie clinging to the roof of her mouth.

Ward sucked his bottom lip between his teeth, his features twisted with worry. He expected her to pass on the offer. Maybe that was the only reason he'd offered.

"Sure," Hazel replied. "Least that way I don't have to worry about you tailing me."

"I wasn't..."

Ear-splitting music drowned out the rest. Hazel started through the crowd, retracing her steps with the hope that Ward would follow. She didn't wait for him. She didn't extend a hand to capture his and pull him along. If he lost sight of her, that was his problem.

The BMW was parked half a block away, on the other side of the street. Gingerly, Hazel propped herself against the shiny hood and settled in to wait. It didn't take long for Ward to catch sight of her when he finally emerged from the club. He stopped in his tracks a few feet away, head tilted at a considering angle.

"You're a little overdressed for a pit babe."

Hazel snorted under her breath. "Dream on."

She thought she spied the twitch of a smile at the corner of Ward's lips as she turned away and wrenched open the passenger side door. Flirting with him was off limits. It shouldn't have come so damn easy. Ward shouldn't have encouraged it.

Then again, if they were big on 'should haves', they wouldn't have wound up in bed together in the first place.

Hazel buckled her seatbelt, heart pitching into her throat as Ward peeled away from the curb with a squeal of tires. In this, he and Dylan were like night and day. Hazel knew which one she should've preferred. She also knew she was grasping at straws if she needed a road test to settle on a favorite.

Ward was the type to blow through yellow lights like a bat out of hell and use his blinkers intermittently. He braked violently and talked as he drove, one hand off the steering wheel at all times. He had a lot of opinions about Hazel's neighborhood, about nearby Los Angeles, the cultural Mecca next door.

Hazel only interrupted to tell him to pull over.

"Why?" he asked, leaning gently on the brakes.

"That's my building over there." She pointed through the windshield to a concrete tower squeezed between two identical others. A gaggle of teenage boys held silent vigil on the cement steps outside, glowering from beneath baseball caps and beanies.

Hazel had seen them before. They were the local flavor, safe simply because they were familiar.

His expression indecipherable, Ward eased up to the curb and killed the engine.

"Do you want to come up?" Dylan's silences were an opportunity to catch her breath, get her feet under her. With Ward, quietude filled her with trepidation about what he'd say next.

He met her gaze. "Better not."

*Right. We might sleep together again.* Hazel smiled and nodded, as though it was little more than a joke. Of course it wouldn't happen again. It wasn't like she lived on a tripwire since she'd met Dylan.

"I can walk you to the door, though," Ward offered tentatively. He slanted a glance through the windshield at the boys who couldn't seem to tear their eyes from the BMW.

"And get another beat down on my behalf?"

"Hey, I put that guy on his back—"

Hazel stepped out of the car to the tune of Ward's indignant protests. "Go home, Prince Charming, before my neighbors send you packing." She ducked down, one hand on the roof of the car and the other gripping the door. "I'll be fine."

The smack of the car door cut off his objection. Whiskey buzzing hot in her bloodstream, Hazel made her way up the sidewalk and to the knot of youths. They looked thirteen and skinny under their baggy shirts and low-slung jeans. In a few years, they'd be on their way to harassing women in bars—like the asshole Ward had knocked out on Hazel's behalf—or hollering at them from tricked-out sedans.

Or maybe they'd land on their feet, grit their teeth and push through college with arrogant jerks like Ward and make something of their lives.

"That your boyfriend, mama?" asked the boldest of the pack.

Hazel followed his gaze to Ward, still parked by the curb.

"He's got a sweet ride," said another boy. He glanced up at Hazel, sizing her up in whatever faint illumination slithered under the busted hallway light.

The jeans and tank top weren't exactly streetwalker attire. She hadn't even bothered putting her face on before she had hightailed it out of the house.

Hazel blew a stray curl off her cheek. "Do me a favor… Stay away from that guy. He's trouble. Mob connections or some shit." One truth for every lie had worked for her before.

She let the shadows of the entryway swallow her up, Ward's gaze hot on the back of her neck.

# Chapter Fourteen

Sadie cornered her in the staff rooms as Hazel was changing out of her uniform. Despite being about a head shorter and thirty pounds lighter, she cut a dangerous portrait standing in the doorframe and blocking Hazel's passage.

"I think I saw this in a porno once," Hazel recalled. Trying to make Sadie blush was a lost battle. Also lost were her attempts to pin her hair up when it was freshly washed or apply makeup in the tiny square mirror glued to the inside of her locker. "What's up?"

"There's an uppity blond asking for you. He said to tell you that Dylan's flight has a half hour delay." Sadie folded her arms across her chest. "Explain."

"He's here?" Hazel's stomach hitched up to her lungs, then promptly dropped into her knees. She'd been hoping to meet Ward outside, partly so she could avoid this kind of grilling, but mostly so he wouldn't see how ill-suited she was for Dylan. Judging by Sadie's quirked eyebrow, she had more immediate obstacles to face. "Oh. That'll be Dylan's roommate."

"The one he's sleeping with."

"Yes."

"The one you don't like."

Hazel resisted the urge to squirm under Sadie's knowing gaze. "It's not that simple." It had been a week ago, when she had resolved never to see him again. Ward was difficult and he was presumptuous, but her body didn't seem to mind that.

As soon as he'd texted her Dylan's flight details, Hazel's pulse had spiked accordingly in anticipation. She found herself chewing her nails, fretful like a schoolgirl.

Then her cell had shrilled with another message — did Hazel want to come with him to the airport?

A question like that deserved only one kind of answer.

"You're starting to sound like him."

Sadie might have meant it as an accusation, but Hazel couldn't resist grinning. She sucked her cheeks in, though, attempting it all the same. "Really? Huh... Well, there are worse things." Dylan had poise and charm. He was a self-made man, a whole rags-to-riches story that would have endeared him to her even if he wasn't also handsome and kind. *And really good in bed.*

"I don't get it," Sadie confessed. "I thought it was over?"

Hazel bit her lip. *I did let you think that.* She'd been wary of telling Sadie the truth — both about prostrating herself on her knees before Dylan and sleeping with his roommate. The snotty one. "It was, but then... I don't know. I think... I think I'd like to try to make it work. I feel good when I'm with him."

"Even — you know?" Sadie canted her head speculatively, the kind of expression that said more than words ever could.

Hazel felt her cheeks grow hot but nodded anyway. "Even that." *Especially that.*

Sadie was not so easily convinced. "I'm worried about you. I went by your place last night and you didn't answer."

"Oh. I wasn't there."

It wasn't the first night she'd taken the car out and driven around aimlessly. It probably wouldn't be the last. She understood, now, why Sadie relied on the open road to make sense of the hubbub inside her skull. There was something about the streets at night—sodium lights streaking the Volvo as she drove, potholes and puddles lending a bass line to whatever soundtrack happened to be playing on the radio—that soothed.

She had driven up Mulholland last night and parked on that stretch of dirt where teenagers went to make out. Soda cans and broken beer bottles crunched under the tires. The city glimmered, sprawling in the valley at her feet.

She'd been tempted to ask Ward to join her. She hadn't.

"No kidding." Sadie scraped her Converse back and forth across the bare cement floor. "I know you're all grown-up and supposed to know what you're doing with your life—"

"I do," Hazel interjected, frowning. She wasn't in the mood for *that* conversation. She didn't have the time, either, even if Dylan was running late.

Undaunted, Sadie steamrolled her objection. "Think about the chances you're taking. These guys... They're in a different league. Tesla and BMW league. You and I barely share a twenty-year-old junk heap." There was something poignant and earnest in her voice—the same kind of something that Hazel usually injected into her pleas. *Don't drive so fast. Don't take so many chances.* That alone kept Hazel from shutting her down. Sadie scowled at the floor. "I don't want to see you get hurt."

"Trust me," Hazel implored. "I won't."

"Do you ever believe me, when *I* say that?"

It was a good point, but it rankled all the same. "If I wanted to be a bitch, I'd say your track record and mine are a *little* different..."

"If?" Sadie sneered. "Just say it. You think I should trust you because you're a goody-goody."

"Okay. Yes."

They stared at each other for a long beat. Eventually, Sadie nodded. The neon overhead flickered too much to guess whether she was conceding defeat or simply retiring the topic.

"Did you see the invites for the reunion?"

Hazel hummed a note of acquiescence. "Rhonda sent one."

"Nice of her." Sadie's tone suggested the opposite.

"Are you thinking of going?" Unlike Hazel, Sadie had pushed through her English degree and come out swinging.

It wasn't her fault that the economy had gone to shit by the time she graduated.

Sadie hitched her shoulders. "It's ten years... I'm a little curious to see how everyone made out."

"I don't blame you."

"We could go together," Sadie started to say, her face falling before she made it halfway through the suggestion. "Oh. Do you think he'll—?"

Hazel pinched her lips. "Probably."

"All the more reason to go. We could key his car. Spill punch on his date..." Sadie smiled ruefully. "Or not. I still think you're making a mistake with Dylan.

My two cents." She held up her hands when Hazel blew out a long, frustrated breath. "I'm going, I'm going." She left the same way she'd come — silently, without a word of apology or goodbye.

*We don't all land on our feet, Sadie. Thanks for reminding me I have shit luck.*

Hazel yanked the elastic scrunchie free of her ponytail and shook out her curls with a hand. Her hair crinkled around her shoulders in unruly ringlets and fluttered in the faint breeze as soon as she set foot into the grease-scented heat of the diner.

She found Ward at the counter, poring over his cell.

"Hey." She approached cautiously, like a snake charmer with an unknown specimen. It wasn't just Ward she felt she didn't know here. After their last tête-à-tête, they hadn't really had a chance to go over the rules of engagement in a public place. Worse, she could feel Sadie watching them out of the corner of her eye. "Ready?"

Ward slid off the bar stool. "You look lovely. Dylan is a lucky man."

He turned for the door before Hazel could puzzle out the acerbic edge in his voice. He didn't quite storm out, but his strides were long and fast. Coming up on the far side of an eight hour shift, Hazel could barely keep up.

"I thought you told Sadie we had time?" she called after him.

"There may be traffic."

"Or there may not. Ward, what the hell?" She caught him by the sleeve of his linen suit, her grip tight, leaving him a choice between hundreds of dollars' worth of sartorial damage or turning to face her.

He picked the latter, twisting around. By the end of that quarter turn, he was once again polished and remote. His expression was set, mask firmly in place — not unlike that night at the club, before regret had gotten the better of him. Before he'd come to Hazel's rescue when she'd called him.

She ignored his scowl. "What's up?"

"Why should anything be up?" he shot back archly.

"Really? We're going to do this now?" Hazel told herself to bite her tongue, to think before she spoke. It was useless, in the end. "You're still sore about what happened? I thought we settled things…"

Ward scoffed.

*Fine, if that's the game you want to play.*

"Is it the dress?" Hazel wheedled. It was borderline see-through and white, and Hazel had been self-conscious since she'd bought it. The thought of all those 'how to dress right for your body type' magazine articles being right filled her with anxiety. But that wasn't what drove her to this line of questioning. "If you're ashamed to be seen with me…"

"Where did you get that dumb idea?"

"You took one look at me in there and said Dylan was a lucky guy. Sounds like you're passing me off to him like a collection plate." *Like you did at the loft, with that bullshit about plying me with liquor so I'd sleep with you.* "Is that it?"

She didn't think so, but if the seclusion of the past few days had confirmed anything at all, it was that Ward operated best in the narrow wedges between guilt and insecurity.

The only way to get anything real out of him was to press where it hurt.

Ward rolled his shoulders as though brushing her off. "We're going to be late."

Hazel weighed the possibility of digging her heels in and telling Ward they weren't going anywhere until they settled this. She thought better of it. There was a good chance that Ward would just head to the airport on his own. He didn't need Hazel to tag along.

"Fine," she sighed. "Lead the way." *So much for trying to make it work.*

\* \* \* \*

LAX spread out before them in a tangle of concrete. Alphabetized lanes that Hazel vaguely recalled from her last jaunt to Missouri assumed they knew where they were going.

Ward seemed nonplussed by the labyrinthine layout. He checked his phone periodically, flight tracker refreshing for news of Dylan's impending arrival, but mostly he seemed to rely on gut instinct and prior experience.

Perhaps he'd driven Dylan to and from the airport before. Perhaps he often flew out of California himself. Either was possible, but Hazel didn't ask and Ward showed no inclination to make conversation with her.

They found a parking spot in silence and marched, also in silence, into the terminal. Hazel thought she'd just about hit the limit of what she was willing to put up with when Ward jerked a finger toward the escalators. "Would you like some coffee?" He was still brooding, but good manners compelled him to ask.

Hazel had never thought she'd be grateful to the one percent for anything, but drilling civility into their offspring came in handy.

"Yeah, sure."

They found a coffee shop on the arrivals level. Ward huffed and puffed a little because it wasn't a Starbucks.

"I don't mind," Hazel told him, meaning every word. She didn't tell him that Starbucks was her rainy day treat, her break-up cure. He'd probably think it was pathetic. "Does Dylan know?" she asked as they stood in line to get their coffees.

"That you came, too? No, I thought you wanted it to be a surprise…"

"I did. I do." Hazel spared a glance to the press of bodies, men and women checking monitors and scoring furrows into the buffed, utilitarian floors with their pacing. "I'm not talking about the welcome committee."

Ward was too sharp-witted not to catch her drift. "Ah." A wrinkle deepened the crease between his eyebrows. He glanced away. "No. He still doesn't. I wasn't sure that you wanted him to hear it from me."

"I thought you two were best friends." *I thought you were planning on throwing yourself on that sword, like a righteous asshole.*

"We are."

"And you won't tell him there's a good chance the woman he's dating is a slut?" Hazel had been called worse things long before she started working at Marco's. Drunks and entitled clientele came with the territory in her profession.

Providentially, Marco didn't put up with that kind of talk and he was pretty good about evicting troublemakers. Along the way, both Hazel and Sadie had developed thick skins. They came in handy sometimes — like now, as Ward sneered at her over the bridge of his nose.

"Still trying to make me into the villain?"

"I don't know what fairy tales your mom read to you, but the princess doesn't usually screw the villain while the prince is away..." *Meeting his birth parents.*

Somehow Dylan's situation didn't lend itself to flippancy. Hazel still wasn't sure she was meant to know the details. She boxed the thought, made a ribbon of her reservations and tied them around it.

"Tell me that what happened between us didn't mean anything and I'll drop it for good," she contended. "You can tell Dylan whatever trumped-up version of the truth you like. I won't get in the way of your self-flagellation."

Ward met her gaze, cool and composed, as though the blood in his veins was so blue it had turned to ice.

"It didn't mean a thing," he said, perfectly level and controlled. Nothing at all like he'd sounded when he lay curled around Hazel, both of them sticky with sweat, his arm flung carelessly around her waist and his lips tracing patterns from her nape to the jut of her shoulder.

Hazel smiled, too, just as measured, and let her Midwestern brogue stretch two syllables out into a drawling third. "Bullshit."

\* \* \* \*

When Dylan emerged through the arrivals gate with the other passengers, Hazel's heart briefly forgot how to operate. The noise level in the hall went from quiet buzzing to nervous hum as friends and families and booked-in-advance chauffeurs waiting to pick up their quarry were suddenly flung into a flurry of activity. Hazel had no trouble hearing each thump of her pulse as it whooshed in her ears.

It got even louder when Dylan glanced their way.

His gaze found Ward, first, and his features relaxed into a smile at once relieved and exhausted. Then he saw Hazel. He stopped smiling.

Not knowing what to do, Hazel raised her hand in a nominal wave. She had the horrible feeling that if he could, Dylan would have sooner turned back than advance the rest of the way to meet them.

The last time they spoke, Dylan had asked her to take his absence to consider what she wanted — if anything — from a relationship with him. But that was two weeks ago. Men like Dylan could live entire lifetimes in two weeks.

"I almost thought they'd keep you," Ward taunted in lieu of greeting. "Well, I *hoped.*"

"So you could steal my girl?" Dylan's eyes darted from Ward to Hazel and back, corners crinkling in amusement.

Hazel winced. "Let's not get ahead of ourselves..."

She hesitated for only an instant before rising on tiptoe and pressing a chaste kiss to Dylan's cheek. The thirteen hour flight had done nothing to coarsen the baby-smooth texture of his skin. He even smelled good. Hazel suppressed another flood of insecurity for the white peasant dress and the unbound hair. She probably looked like she'd just emerged from Woodstock — and that was fine. That was okay. She wasn't going to change herself for any guy, let alone two.

"I didn't expect to see you," Dylan said. "Here, I mean. I was planning on calling you tonight, of course — "

"Well, now you don't have to." Ward stuck his hands in his pockets. "Shall we? I know I have money to throw around, but it irks me to pay extra for parking." He set out without waiting for confirmation.

Seeing as he had the car keys, Hazel judged it wise to follow.

She didn't expect to feel Dylan slot his hand into hers as they navigated the crowded hall, much less have him lean in to ask, "What's gotten into him?"

Ward's shoulders were a perfect horizontal line. His gray suit jacket fluttered unbuttoned against his sides. He was trying very hard to be nonchalant about Dylan's return. A week ago, Hazel might have believed it. She was starting to get wise to the many faces of Ward Parrish, so she felt confident when she turned to Dylan with the answer.

"He's being his usual sunny self. What else?"

Dylan rewarded her with a smile, but it was soft and uncertain. The dynamic between him and Ward was completely unlike anything that Hazel had witnessed before. Ward was meant to be the master of ceremonies and Dylan his loyal but long-suffering aide. Not the other way around.

Gloom hung over them until it finally crystallized as they crowded around the BMW.

Ward popped the trunk as Dylan collapsed his trolley suitcase and prepared to slot it in.

"So Ward and I had sex," Hazel blurted out. She could have couched it in euphemism—spent the night, got to know each other a little better, explored the second story of the loft, tripped and landed with Tab A in Slot B—but none suited her purpose so well.

Ward's glare could have melted the polar ice caps. He froze with one hand on the hood of the car, his jangling keychain in the other. He suddenly seemed a little pallid too, nostrils flaring as he blew out a long breath.

In the face of his palpable aggravation, Hazel was glad that Dylan stood between them, albeit grunting with effort. He scraped his palms together once he'd successfully levered the suitcase into place. "I thought something was up... How was it?"

"What?" Hazel asked, Ward not far behind.

But Dylan was insouciant. "Did you enjoy it?" He turned slowly to give Hazel his undivided attention. For some ungodly reason, that was more unsettling than if he'd turned red with ill-suppressed rage. "Did he show you a good time?"

Hazel thought back to Ward's hands digging bruises into her hips, his lips tracing runes into her shoulder. "Yes," she breathed. She could scent Dylan's cologne as a sticky, warm current blew through the parking lot. She swayed a little toward him, snared.

"Good." Dylan reached up and brushed a stray lock of hair behind her ear. "He can be a little rough."

"Standing right here," Ward said and emphatically cleared his throat.

"Yes... And this explains that giant stick up your ass."

Ward shifted his weight, but his rambling irritation was fast becoming an afterthought. "Don't get snippy with me, Mr. Five Hundred Dollar Shoes."

"They're knock-offs," Dylan shot back. He was still watching Hazel, the shallow curve of a smile painted on his lips. "Are you okay?"

She knew what he was asking — not about the sex, but their incipient relationship, the odds of venturing into something more complicated than the friends-with-benefits routine he seemed to favor. Hazel had been wondering as much herself ever since he told her about his 'roommate'. Now she knew firsthand that Ward wasn't the easiest person to live with. Neither was she.

"We'll need ground rules," Hazel said. "But yeah... I want to give it a shot."

Dylan's grin was blinding and warm, and liable to make her say and do many stupid things if she didn't inoculate somehow against its power.

"Then let's go home. Ward, you're driving."

"Yes, sir," Ward drawled, rolling his eyes. Hazel didn't know him very well and it might have been a trick of the light, but she had the unshakeable suspicion that he was *relieved* as they all piled together into the BMW.

She sat in the back, the pleats in her white dress billowing in the artificial breeze from the AC. Once in a while, her gaze drifted to the clutch, where Dylan had folded his hand over Ward's.

# Chapter Fifteen

Dylan begged off for a shower as soon as they stepped through the loft door. Hazel watched his suitcase, a solitary rectangle forgotten by the door, and wondered what he'd found in Shanghai, if his trip had been fruitful. She thought about asking Ward, but he was back to brooding as he mixed a cocktail that seemed to involve more gin than tonic.

"Are you sure that's wise?" Hazel asked, resting one arm on the backrest of the couch.

Ward pivoted to face her, a slice of lime in hand. "I won't tell if you don't."

A week ago, Hazel would've taken that for an unsubtle threat. It was becoming harder and harder to believe him capable. *Terrible thing, letting your lust play judge of character...*

"Share and I won't be tempted," Hazel challenged.

"After your performance at the airport, I have trouble believing you know the meaning of discretion." The rebuke was earned, but it did nothing to stop Hazel from bristling.

"Next time I promise to let you hang yourself like a good little martyr."

"Good."

"Fine."

Ward handed her a cocktail with barely any kick and no lime. Like all high class bullies, he fought his wars through petty shenanigans. Hazel would've liked to see him sink or swim in her old high school, particularly when he volleyed, "Don't you need to get back to waiting tables?"

His barbed remarks were by far the worst thing about him. "You know," Hazel retorted, "if you weren't so pretty, you'd be wearing my drink right now."

"It was a simple question," Ward defended, but he stepped out of her reach at the threat. He rounded the couch, the setting sun at his back.

"No, it wasn't. If you don't want me here—"

"Did I say that?"

Hazel rolled her eyes. "Better make up your mind. Dylan might put up with the passive aggressive crap, but I'm not going to." It was a chancy threat, but if Dylan wanted her to stick around, then Ward's fickle moods would have to settle. And fast.

"Here I thought that's what a good submissive is supposed to do," Ward said. "Put up. Put out," he added, smirking at the symmetry.

"Who says I'm a good submissive?" Her hackles raised, Hazel sidestepped the part where she accepted the label in the first place.

"I did," Dylan replied from the far end of the living room. He was pink from the shower, shiny black hair curling handsomely at his nape. He hadn't deigned to put pants on, so the V of his hips was all too visible over the edge of a terrycloth towel.

He was a vision, but even handsome and half naked, Dylan couldn't distract Hazel's attention from a more immediate problem. "You *discussed* me with him?"

"Not in detail."

"Christ." Hazel took a sip of her drink. It was as bitter as she'd feared. The absence of lime to elevate the taste made itself felt.

"I'm sure you discussed me with Sadie — and possibly Ward."

"That's not —" She caught herself before she finished uttering the lie. "Okay, fine. It's true we mentioned you, but —"

"It's no different," Dylan insisted. He padded barefoot across the hardwood floor and snagged Ward's glass out of his hands.

"It's just soda water," Ward started to protest. He threw up his hands when Dylan took a sip. "I hate living with a teetotaler."

"And yet you love living with *me*." Dylan's smile was generous and confident, and Hazel knew she'd go far to make him look at her like that.

Ward scoffed, but the barest trace of a grin tensed the corners of his lips, giving away the lie. He recovered his glass when Dylan held it out.

"What's your deal with alcohol?" Hazel felt compelled to ask.

"I don't have a 'deal' with alcohol," Dylan countered. The way he stood there, between the glare of sunlight and fully dressed, smirking Ward was very avenging angel — or Abercrombie model. He was limned in gold, his body compact and distracting — almost as much as his voice when he added, "Except before I sleep with someone."

Hazel gulped.

"Ambitious," Ward teased. "What happened to the jetlag?"

"I slept on the plane. Besides, I'll have you there to guide me if I slip up, won't I? Since you two are already acquainted, it seems only fair not to exclude anyone..."

Both Ward and Hazel sucked in a breath at that. Ward in particular seemed thrown by the suggestion. "Shouldn't you ask the lady what she wants first?" he deflected.

It took Hazel a long moment to puzzle out the flow of influence between them. She'd mistakenly believed that Ward was pulling Dylan's strings. Maybe that was true ten years back, when they were still in college and Dylan had something to prove. The balance of power had shifted since.

Dylan palmed Ward's cheek in a broad, capable hand—Hazel knew just how capable from firsthand experience. Ward leaned into it, his eyes drooping shut. He was by far the most clothed person in the room and yet he shivered visibly when Dylan pulled away.

"What do you think, Hazel?"

The sound of her name broke Hazel from the trance she'd fallen under. "What?"

"Do you want to be with the two of us? Or one...? Or neither...?"

"Yeah." Hazel scratched absently at her knee, then stopped short when she noticed Dylan's gaze following the motion of her fingers. She hitched her hem up a little and he smiled. God, he had a smile to make a girl do crazy, crazy things. "But I meant it about the rules." She darted a glance at Ward, relieved when she didn't find him smirking, rolling his eyes, or just generally acting derisive.

Dylan rested both hands on the back of the Barcelona chair. "I'm listening."

She'd never done this pre-emptively. Usually it was a matter of dismissing what she didn't like as an evening wore on—and most of her one-night stands had been too vanilla to hit hard limits. The ones who *did*, she often got off with hastily then sent on their way. It had been years since she had attempted anything more substantial. And now here she was, faced with the real possibility of going down the rabbit hole again, with both Dylan *and* Ward.

A shiver rippled across her skin in anticipation.

"No blindfolds. No gags." Hazel took a shuddering breath. The living room was warm and yet she felt chilled all of a sudden, a mixture of anticipation and anxiety roiling in her gut. "If I ask you to stop, you stop."

"Always," Dylan promised and though he was smiling softly, his gaze was firm and self-assured. He meant it.

"Your turn."

Dylan arched an eyebrow. "My rules for you?"

"For both of us," Hazel corrected. She didn't know what their relationship was like when she wasn't around, but Ward certainly lugged his guilt around like a ball and chain.

Dylan took a moment to think. "If you want something, you ask for it."

"That's it?"

He shrugged. "That's all I need."

"What about letting me tie you up?" Ward interjected. "Is there a rule for that?"

Dylan shook his head. "Not unless you have one…"

"I do, actually." Ward set his glass down on the coffee table. The gin and tonic swished within, a churning sea in a crystal tumbler. "No recordings of any kind. What happens in this apartment stays here."

He very pointedly didn't meet Hazel's eyes—not even when Dylan frowned in confusion—and she felt a swell of tenderness at the thought that he'd bring that up for her sake.

And it had to be for her sake, because he had nothing to lose from laying out his sexual proclivities for the world to see.

*Look at that. The Tin Man has a heart.*

"I'd say that settles it." Hazel rose from the couch. "Don't you?" She tried to be elegant about it. She tried to be sultry. But with every step that brought her closer to Dylan's bedroom, she felt her heart pound harshly in her ears. What was she doing? What if this backfired?

What if Dylan and Ward discarded her like Sadie had warned?

Hazel seized the hem of her dress with both hands and yanked it over her head, shivering despite the balmy heat. She knew this room, this bed. Her gaze strayed to the door of the playroom, but she didn't move toward it. If Dylan wanted her in there, he'd tell her.

She didn't turn at the sound of bare feet slapping the hardwood floor.

"Now *this* is a sight to come home to," Dylan breathed softly.

Hazel slid her bra straps down—*in for a penny*—and swiftly discarded the scrap of reinforced silk. She hooked two fingers in the waistband of her panties, intending to get the unveiling over with before she lost her nerve, only to feel Dylan's hands settle over hers.

"Let me," he purred.

So Hazel did. She slid her palms over her belly, up the ridges of her ribcage and the swell of her breasts. Her nipples peaked beneath her fingertips. She trembled as Dylan bade her step out of her underwear, but nowhere near as badly as she did when he kissed the swell of her hip or traced his fingertips along the backs of her knees.

"Do you remember the stoplight?"

"Yes." *Vaguely.* It wasn't his fault. She just had a hard time concentrating when he was tracing her skin with feather-light caresses—an affliction worsened by the click of Ward's footfalls.

"Put this on," Ward said briskly and tossed something metallic onto the perfectly made bed.

Hazel picked up the chain. It attached to a strip of coiled leather at one end and a collar at the other, the latter secured with a steel buckle.

"You don't have to," Dylan put in, his breaths fanning across her shoulder as she straightened. "But you'd look hot wearing it."

"I wouldn't be here if I didn't have a healthy appreciation for props..."

That said, it still took her a minute to slide the collar on and secure it, her fingers big and clumsy around the buckle. Dylan didn't reach up to help her. She wondered if that had to do with Ward's presence in the room—or, better yet, his silence. She cinched it reasonably loose, swallowing a couple of times just to feel the leather pull against her throat. "What do you want me to do with the lead?" she asked, chest rattling. The length of chain dangled uselessly between her breasts, leather handgrip brushing her inner thigh.

Dylan didn't answer, but he turned her a little so Ward could take hold of the lead. In the process, he stroked the back of his pale hand along her sex. Hazel gasped. There was no injunction against speaking and yet the moment felt so charged that she was hesitant to break the silence.

"On your knees," Ward commanded. His features were set with obvious intent, but the heat in his black eyes chased away all sense of dread.

Hazel steadied herself with a hand on the bed as she sank down, never dropping his gaze. She wanted him to tell her it was a faux pas. She wanted those strong, heavy hands of his in her hair, steering her. Her breath caught when he raised one, but it wasn't to strike her.

Dylan's towel brushed her ankle as it came undone and fell to the floor. She knew immediately what Ward intended and she was turning before he could beckon Dylan closer. He was already erect and flushed with blood when she took hold of him.

"Greedy," Dylan rasped. He flexed his fists at his sides, the muscles in his abdomen drawing taut. "Fuck, your hands are cold."

"Oh, I'm sorry —"

"He likes it," Ward said from high over her right shoulder. He was rummaging for something in the bedside drawer, the sound vague but purposeful. Hazel couldn't puzzle it out until he pressed a condom into her hands.

"I'm not crazy about sucking latex…"

"And I'm not crazy about STDs," Ward countered. "Put it on."

"That's becoming a familiar refrain," Dylan chuckled. He had the good grace to sound a little choked.

Hazel glanced up at him as she tore the condom out of its wrapper and slid it delicately down his cock. She was gratified when he coiled a hand into her hair to pull her forward, impatience winning out.

*That's it. Use me.*

She wasn't going to think about why she needed it so badly or worry that she was giving Dylan and Ward too much power over her. As she parted her lips around the head of Dylan's erection, she found her thoughts leaching like water through a sieve.

Dylan was heavy and hot on her tongue, her lips sealed tight around his shaft, and she reveled in the aborted, near-imperceptible movement of his hips as he struggled not to thrust forward. His exhales were guttural moans, pleasure writ in the tight pull of his fingers in her hair. "That's it," he growled. "Just like that."

She would have obliged gladly, if Ward didn't pick that precise moment to pull lightly on the lead, dragging her back. The collar tugged around her throat, an unpleasant sensation, and Hazel slid off, licking her lips.

"I thought you wanted —"

"I didn't say you could get him off," Ward interjected. She could hear the suppressed laughter in his voice.

"Sadist," Dylan breathed fondly.

The warmth in his voice settled Hazel's bourgeoning anxiety.

"I'll let you have more if you remember not to make him come," Ward murmured. "Can you do that, Hazel?" The way he phrased it made the question sound innocent and fair, a matter of choice.

Hazel didn't want *choice*. She licked her lips and nodded, ducking her head to take as much of Dylan into her mouth as she could. His cock was longer than Ward's and though slightly thinner, it still filled her mouth perfectly. She knew what would happen when she worked her throat muscles around him.

A sharp, almost pained noise erupted from his chest.

This time the pull on the collar was sudden and merciless, coupled with a hand in Hazel's hair to drag her off Dylan. Ward forced her gaze to his. "What did I just say?"

"I wasn't paying attention?" Hazel retorted, defiant.

She loved the spark of anger in Ward's gaze almost as much as the answering, disbelieving guffaw she heard from Dylan. *How's that for a good submissive?*

"You want to suck cock? Fine." Ward undid the zipper on his slacks one-handed and fumbled for his erection. Another condom. Another hiss of torn foil. Ward's dexterity was a thing of beauty — much like the raised tendons in his wrist as he gripped the base of his dick.

Hazel was ready when he pulled her to him, her mouth watering in anticipation. She was ready for the brutal scrape of the collar around her neck and the eye-watering pressure in the back of her throat.

What she didn't anticipate was that Dylan would take that moment to crouch down and palm her breasts. A zing of pleasure skittered beneath her skin, distracting her with its heat and its promise of more, more, more. She forgot to breathe through her nose for a moment.

The cough that rattled free of her lungs would've been mortifying if Hazel could have still thought in those terms. Ward canted his hips back, letting her catch her breath. "Is this what you want? Do you need to be punished, you greedy little slut?" His grip on her hair was as rough as Dylan's fingers pinching her nipples. And Hazel was caught between them, a fish on a line, wriggling helplessly.

"He asked you a question," Dylan purred, the good cop to Ward's bad. "Don't you think it's polite to answer?"

"Yes."

"Yes, what?"

"Yes, I need..." Hazel sucked in breath after harsh breath, her throat scraped raw. "I need to be punished. I need this."

Ward gripped his member by the root and nudged it past her lips again, as though to silence her. With his fist in the way, Hazel couldn't take as much as before. She couldn't choke on it, either. *Good thinking.*

"God, that's sexy," Dylan chuckled. "You look right at home with a cock in your mouth, sweetheart."

*That's so demeaning* was Hazel's first, foggy thought. Her second was *fuck, that's so hot.*

Dylan didn't stop there. His talented hands roamed—restlessly, it seemed to Hazel, then with purpose. When he slid a fingertip between her folds, she could barely resist arching her hips to demand more. But that wasn't how this game was played. As soon as she bucked, Dylan removed his hand completely and went back to kneading her breasts. The disconnect between his rough hands and his heartrendingly tender kisses was so powerful that Hazel felt like there were two of her—one who deserved a gentle hand and one who had earned her penance.

Both were at Ward's mercy when he finally backed off.

"On the bed," he growled and if Hazel had once thought that Dylan's bedroom voice was capable of bringing her to heel with a single word, then she hadn't considered who he'd studied under.

She nearly got tangled in the chain in her haste, but with a helping hand from Ward, Hazel landed on her back, knees still hooked over the edge of the bed. She yelped when Dylan hauled her back to him by the ankles.

"You think she's earned a reward?" Ward asked conversationally.

"Who says it's a reward?" Dylan's eyes gleamed as he pressed a bite into the crease of Hazel's hip.

She knew better than to try to wiggle out from under him. Ragged breaths scraped the inside of her throat when he veered closer and closer to her sex, anticipation mounting. Behind her breastbone, her heart was a frantic drum marking time. She was as unprepared for the first swipe of Dylan's tongue as she was for the bed dipping when Ward dropped down to the mattress beside her.

He had undressed hastily, not much of a strip show. The sight of him naked and prowling toward her tugged a moan from Hazel's throat. She reached for him blindly, greedily, hooking both hands around his shoulders as their lips met. She already knew that Ward didn't kiss like Dylan. He didn't seem to believe in taking his time. He was all conquest and teeth, palming her cheek with one hand and fisting the metal chain with the other. The links clicked and jangled together, a reminder of what was at stake.

"Look at him," Ward ordered. "I know he can eat pussy well. You should appreciate every facet of his hard work, don't you think?" He glanced down her body himself, gaze fastening to the crown of Dylan's head as he fucked her with his tongue. "Look," he urged again, when Hazel was slow to obey.

He slid a hand behind her nape, propping her up so she'd get a good view of Dylan's greedy, noisy slurping.

As if she needed visual proof. Every stroke of his tongue was like a lash, at once sweet and agonizing. Every press of his fingers into her cunt had her choking back pleas for more, for harder. She knew what he was doing to her — he'd done it before.

"Drives me crazy when you — *yes*," Hazel hissed, "right there. Oh, fuck —"

She groped for purchase on the bed sheets and somehow found Ward's thigh instead. He didn't so much as flinch when she dug her nails into his flesh.

"Getting close, aren't you?" Ward hooked a fingertip beneath the collar. "Going to come all over his tongue?"

Hazel nodded frantically. She could taste her climax. It was building at her core, fueled by each tantalizing stroke, each whisper.

"Stop," Ward said. To her great horror, Dylan immediately pulled away.

A whine tore from Hazel's chest. "*Fuck.* Why?"

"I didn't say you could come, did I?"

*You sound like him.* It wasn't such a terrible thing. Dylan, after all, was running his hands in soothing circles over her thighs. That didn't stop Hazel from glaring up at Ward. He looked good up there, lips crimson from kissing, sunlight catching on his blond hair.

Hazel boldly walked her fingers up his thigh to the curve of his dick. "You gonna make me choose?" Her words were slightly slurred. She hoped he didn't mind.

"No." Ward caught her wrist. "Because you'll take us both."

Dylan crawled up onto the bed with them, his lips curled into a knowing grin. "You'd like that, wouldn't you? You're gushing wet just at the thought..." He would know. He had two fingers inside her, scissoring gently along the tight clutch of sensitive muscle.

Hazel arched beneath him, a moan building in her throat. She didn't have to wait long. Dylan seized hold of her hips and pressed in slowly and gently, entering her with just the head of his erection. She clenched around him all the same, mounting anticipation getting the better of her.

"Relax," Dylan crooned. "You'll enjoy this."

"She already is," Ward said, practically reading her mind.

It was just as well that he did the talking because that part of Hazel's brain had checked out by the time Dylan settled above her.

He nuzzled at her lips until she opened her mouth to him. Then they were kissing—or rather he was kissing her—and Hazel could hear someone panting for breath but it didn't occur to her that those wheezing noises were coming from her own throat until Dylan pulled back to watch her.

"Quit screwing around and fuck her," Ward grunted. "You know you want to."

Dylan lost the gentle, tender pace almost at once. Hazel ran her hands over his flanks reverently, so caught up in the pistoning movement of his hips and the intense concentration painted on his features that she didn't feel Ward slip away until he was sliding something cold and tight around her wrists.

It was the leather cuffs Dylan had used on her in the playroom.

Ward gripped the chain with one hand, forcing her arms above her head. "There's more where that came from."

"God, I hope so," Hazel blurted out. Her face was already so hot that she didn't think she could blush redder if she tried.

Dylan slammed his hips into hers, curbing that thought before it consumed her. "Fuck, this feels so good... She's so *tight*."

"I know," said Ward, a cocksure twist to his mouth. "Fuck her hard and don't stop until you come. She can take it."

Hazel wasn't so sure, but she didn't disagree. The harsh pounding gave her just enough friction to keep her lucid and aware of her surroundings. Everything else was Dylan and Ward and their hands sweetly bruising her tender flesh. She couldn't smother her moans as she felt herself nearing the brink of release. Dylan wasn't far behind. He dug his fingers into her thighs and thrust deep once, twice, before coming with a throaty growl.

Even flushed a deep crimson and shaking like a leaf, he was still careful as he curled over her.

"Ngh," Hazel protested, rocking her hips beneath his as best she could. She was so close and it was so unfair—

"My turn," Ward rasped.

He and Dylan exchanged places carefully, with Dylan holding the condom fast to the base of his cock as he withdrew.

Hazel's inner muscles contracted around thin air, her thwarted orgasm ebbing away like a floundering storm. There was no one to stop her bringing her bound hands to her cunt.

Dylan chuckled when he saw. Ward smirked with half a mouth.

"You do it, then," he snickered, "if you're so desperate." His stiff length gave him away despite the chilling edge in his voice.

Flustered, Hazel held his gaze as she struggled to align them. It was challenging to do it blind, but every delay only served to torment them both. *Turn around is fair play…*

Ward filled her in one swift thrust, hoisting her ankles over his shoulders as pressed in deep. It hurt. Dylan had coaxed her open with fingers and cock, and Hazel was so wet that Ward should have slipped in easy, but it hurt a little all the same. Hazel cried out, the sound cutting off abruptly when she felt someone snag the chain in their hand.

"This is punishment," Dylan murmured. "Or did you think he forgot?"

"Fuck." Her eyes squeezed nearly completely shut, she could only see a sliver of Dylan's face in the blinding glow of light. It was enough to know that he was smirking.

*You're enjoying this.*

Ward scraped a fingertip over her clit.

*Hell, I'm enjoying it, too.*

Despite the raw, near-painful drag of friction, despite the frustration that accompanied her ruined orgasms, Hazel found herself soaring, tethered to her body only by the flimsiest of hooks. Ward rode her hard, seeking his own pleasure and caring nothing for her own. His flushed face was set in a grimace, teeth bared and eyes rooted to hers, and that alone could have sent her careering over the edge.

Instead, she cried out as Ward pinched the engorged nubbin of her clit tight between thumb and forefinger. "Not yet."

Hazel felt tears leak into her hair as he drove his hips faster and faster, racing toward his high.

"*Now.*"

Permission was perfunctory. As blood flowed back into her compressed flesh, Hazel bucked against the bed, thrashing as orgasm rode her hard. She cried out, tension building to an unfathomable crescendo. Then pleasure took over, wave after wave of heat rippling across her skin as she sank, boneless, into the bedclothes.

She had no memory of Ward withdrawing and lowering her legs to the mattress. When she glanced down a minute or an hour later, he was rubbing her feet between his hands, so gentle that it might have been contrition animating the tender strokes.

"Aaand she's back," Dylan breathed, a smile in his voice. He was carding fingers through her hair and he grinned when their eyes met. "I'm a little jealous."

"I passed out?"

"For a few seconds."

"I pushed you," Ward said and *he* wasn't smiling. The furrow between his eyebrows had grown to a channel deep enough to fit the Marianas.

Dylan palmed her cheek, forcibly turning her attention back to him. "How are you feeling?"

"Good."

"Anything hurt?"

Hazel flexed toes and fingers. She squirmed a little against the bed sheets. The collar and wristlets were gone, disappeared into whatever toy cupboard the boys used to conceal their torture implements. "I'm a little sore..."

"Not surprised." Dylan stroked his thumb along the curve of her cheek. "Your back's okay?"

"I must seem very fragile to you." Hazel made to sit up, but Dylan pressed a hand between her breasts, keeping her down.

"You don't. Ward is freaking out because no one's ever fainted from the power of his cock before."

"Oh, shut up," Ward groaned under his breath.

"Do they often faint for *you*?" Hazel quipped but she settled back against the mattress as instructed. She could do that much to keep the peace.

"All the time." Dylan propped himself up onto his elbow. "So, if everything was good and nothing hurts *too* much, can you please tell him to calm down and get over here?"

Hazel craned her neck. "He looks calm."

"That's because *I* talked him down. He's holding out on joining us, though." Dylan slid a long-suffering glance down the bed. "He can be trying."

"Ward." Hazel held out a hand. "Come here before Dylan breaks his arm patting himself on the back?"

With the clarity of afterglow and the satisfaction of a worthwhile scene smothering her insecurities, Hazel knew suddenly that it wouldn't be easy to navigate a relationship with two men. They might stand a chance as long as they were all willing to compromise. They already had a lock on sexual chemistry. That was something.

Ward heaved a put-upon sigh and flopped down beside her. His spent dick rested soft and warm against Hazel's thigh.

"You're pretty good at this dominating thing," Hazel breathed, tipping her head against his shoulder.

She had grown used to Ward smirking and scoffing, brushing off anything that so much as flirted with significance. She wouldn't have been surprised to hear him laugh in response.

He didn't. Instead, he brushed her temple with his lips and said, "You, too."

Out of the corner of her eye, Hazel glimpsed Dylan's self-satisfied grin. She let him have this one. There were worse reasons to look smug.

# Epilogue

She woke in a tangle of limbs. The sheets were a jumble of crinkled damask beneath her. Dylan lay on her hair, one hand curled around her breast. Ward had casually flung an arm across her belly as he spooned her from behind. Even soft, his cock was a noticeable bulge against her backside. It spurred all kinds of wayward thoughts.

Hazel had more pressing concerns.

Ward tightened his hold as she made to pry her way loose and he blinked awake with a frown when she persisted.

*It figures he frowns even in his sleep.*

"I'm just going to the bathroom," Hazel reassured him, keeping her voice low so as not to wake Dylan.

Ward took a moment to parse out her words, then nodded and withdrew his hand. It was hard not to miss its warmth.

Hazel scrabbled her way to the foot of the bed on wobbly legs. When she glanced back, Ward had closed his eyes again. Probably feigning sleep, she thought. She was beginning to figure out how his busy mind worked. The things he was afraid of rang oddly familiar.

After using the facilities and washing her hands, Hazel wrapped herself in the terrycloth robe she found on a hook on the back of the door. It was softer than any she owned. She made a mental note to ask Dylan what kind of laundry powder he used. *Later.* When she stepped back into the bedroom, Dylan was tucked neatly into the empty space she'd just vacated, his cheek on Ward's pale shoulder. They looked at once wicked and divine together, moonlight slanting across their bodies and shadows pooling in the few hollows left between them.

It was a shame that she couldn't paint for shit because those two had bodies nude models would kill for. She filed away the thought as she padded out of the room.

She was thirsty and she needed to stretch. Mostly, though, she needed to recoup.

The urge to call Sadie and have some good ol'-fashioned girl talk surged inside her like a craving for chocolate. She rummaged for her phone in her purse and took it over to the couch. It was only nine o'clock. Sadie would still be up.

If Hazel was lucky, tonight would be a quiet night at Marco's and they could talk.

She typed her passcode and swiped to unlock the screen. Her inbox was seventeen missed calls and twenty-two messages deep, all received since the afternoon.

Hazel felt her stomach sink. It settled slightly when she realized that the calls were all from Sadie or Marco's. Nothing from Dunby. No sign that calamity had struck her family. Hazel scrolled to the first message in the queue. It was from Sadie.

*Don't freak out but call me back when you get this.*

The second, in the same vein, pleaded with Hazel to get in touch ASAP. Third and fourth were identical resends. Could be network glitches, Hazel reasoned, trying to keep calm. The fifth message reduced her mental gymnastics to dust.

*He's posting your picture and vid on some gross website. With your number. Call me.*

"Hazel?"

She startled at the sound of Dylan's voice. With the lights out, his shadow blended with the darkness of the room. The dizzying, riotous thoughts clamoring in her skull dimmed in his presence.

"Everything okay?"

"Yeah," she lied. "I was going to get some, uh, some water." Her mouth was thick with cotton, cloying with honey and bile. She had to swallow a couple of times before she could muster enough spit to add, "How did you escape Octopus Man in there?"

"Ward?" Dylan raked a hand through his inky hair. "He's pretending to be fast asleep. If we're not back soon, he'll probably come looking." He didn't seem overly concerned about the prospect.

He padded barefoot and naked into the kitchen, rounding the island to fetch a bottled water from the fridge. "If you need to make a call—"

"I don't." Hazel tossed the phone to the couch, having typed a quick *I'll call you in the morning* to Sadie. She took the water from Dylan's outstretched hand. "There's no middle ground with you, is there?"

Dylan arched an eyebrow.

"Suit and tie or birthday suit."

"Do you have a preference?"

Hazel grinned and let her eyes rake down his body. "I'll get back to you on that."

When she hauled her gaze back to his face, she found him smiling crookedly. Even covered from her knees to her chin, she couldn't help but feel a little self-conscious beneath his stare.

"Thank you," Dylan said.

"I haven't moved any mountains lately."

"For sticking around. For...giving us a chance." It was hard to say if 'us' referred to him and Hazel or him, Hazel *and* Ward. Possibly the latter.

Hazel hitched up a shoulder. "I have fun here. And Ward really likes to cut in, so we're better off including him, anyway." She could see bemusement in the crease of Dylan's brow. "I'll explain some other time. How was Shanghai?"

His expression morphed into one of ill-concealed glee. "Ah... Ward told you, didn't he?"

"Yes." She felt sheepish admitting it, but it wasn't her fault. "I didn't *ask*."

"I imagine not. I wanted to tell you, but—"

"Too intimate, I get it." Hazel held out her hands in surrender. "We're cool."

"I *do* want to tell you. Now that I know you might be, you know, staying in orbit, I want to do all sorts of things... Including talking."

"But not exclusively?"

A shiver raced down Hazel's spine as Dylan slowly shook his head. He watched her intently, as though scouring the deep recesses of her being all the way to that small part of her that wouldn't mind being told to bend over right then and there. Kitchen sex had all the appeal of missionary with the lights out in her apartment, but the loft was different. The exposed brick and the cool granite countertops called to mind decadence and rough, no-holds-barred grappling.

"We should go back to Ward," Dylan suggested.

"Okay…"

"And," Dylan added just as she made to walk away, "if he's up for it, you two can catch me up on whatever else you've been up to these past couple of weeks…"

"What if I'm not up for it?" Hazel asked coquettishly.

"You will be," Dylan retorted, and that sexy, gravelly note in his voice zoomed straight to her core.

She heard him trail her into the bedroom at a leisurely pace, a predator well aware that their prey was cornered. Her pulse spiked in answer.

As predicted, Ward was propped up on his elbows, glaring at the door when they stepped through.

"Someone's cross," Hazel drawled.

"No," Dylan scoffed. "That's his resting face—"

He didn't get another word in before Ward tackled him to the bed.

Hazel watched them wrestle for a moment, an outsider looking in, and promptly decided she didn't have to stand for that.

She let the bathrobe hit the floor.

# About the Author

Helena Maeve has always been globe trotter with a fondness for adventure, but only recently has she started putting to paper the many stories she's collected in her excursions. When she isn't writing erotic romance novels, she can usually be found in an airport or on a plane, furiously penning in her trusty little notebook.

Helena Maeve loves to hear from readers. You can find her contact information, website details and author profile page at http://www.totallybound.com.

Totally Bound Publishing